J. D. RYDER

GONE TO TEXAS

Complete and Unabridged

LINFORD
Leicester

First published in Great Britain in 2010 by
Robert Hale Limited
London

First Linford Edition
published 2011
by arrangement with
Robert Hale Limited
London

British Library CIP Data

Ryder, J. D., *1937 –*
    Gone to Texas.- -(Linford western library)
    1. Western stories.
    2. Large type books.
    I. Title II. Series
    823.9'2–dc22

    ISBN 978–1–4448–0737–0

Published by
F. A. Thorpe (Publishing)
Anstey, Leicestershire

Set by Words & Graphics Ltd.
Anstey, Leicestershire
Printed and bound in Great Britain by
T. J. International Ltd., Padstow, Cornwall

This book is printed on acid-free paper

1

It was clear to me, war made Andrew a killer. Yeah, I know. That's what war is about, killing your enemies. But this was more'n that.

I grew up with Andrew and knew him like he was my brother. That was a very different man than the Andrew that came out of the war, the one most southerners were calling the War Between the States. Anyone that makes it alive comes away from it changed, I'd say, more for some than others.

Now you don't have to say it, there was a lot of bad things come out of that war and I know it. First-hand I know it. And I'm sure you ain't really interested in what I got to say about it either, but my story does work around to where it just might have to do with you and yours. So if you'd allow, I'd like to recount it. Somewhere along the way

1

you'll see where I'm going with it.

Now, back to killing people. We all did what we had to do, all us soldiers. Take me for example; I done my share of killing just like Andy did and was even wounded in the same battle as him, but after that, things was different. Guess maybe getting shot in the leg is not the same as being hit in the head.

There'd been a lot of good old boys wearing the makeshift uniform of the Southern Army in what Pa called the War of Rebellion killed and a lot more wounded. Me'n Andy hadn't been in the war very long, neither. I don't guess the thought of my getting shot or even killed ever come into my thinking.

I don't recall what I was doing when I was hit. One minute I was standing beside a tree aiming my rifle at the blue coats coming up the hill at us, waiting for the signal to fire, and the next I was down clutching at my knee. Lightning was my first thought. I'd been struck by lightning and my knee was all ablaze. Oh, it hurt, I'll tell you and I probably

yelled a mite, but I don't know.

Nobody paid me any mind, not at first. The order had come down and everybody was busy shooting and yelling their own selves. I tried to reach my rifle, I really did, but I couldn't let go my leg. When they came to get me and all the others what was wounded, I'd forgot all about my rifle. Far as I know it's still there on that hillside ready to shoot someone. Only someone shot me first.

Just like all the others wounded in that battle, I was hauled back down to our lines on a canvas stretcher. A tent had been set up to serve as a field hospital. Two rows of cots lined the tent and what doctors there was went up one side and down the other, doing what they could. As a bed comes empty, another man was brought in.

I lay outside on a blanket for a long time, holding on to my leg to keep it from twitching. The hurt was something awful.

When the doctor got to me, he

3

simply cut a big hole in my pants leg and poked at the wound. I looked at it too. It looked like the bullet went right through my knee bone. I glanced up in time to see that the doctor was reaching for his saw. I decided that lying back and letting him cut my leg off wasn't the best thing to do. I'd seen the pile of arms and legs outside and didn't want part of me out there. They didn't have any chloroform or even a bit of whiskey, and the teeth on that bloody saw didn't look none too sharp. I let out an argument and he stopped.

'Boy,' he said, not even taking the chewed-up cigar butt from his mouth, 'I haven't the time to fight you over this. Either I amputate or that leg will turn poison and kill you. Now let me get on with it, hear?'

Well, if he was in that big a hurry, I told him, then just pass me by and get on to helping the next soldier. I wasn't giving up any of my legs. No sir.

'I don't have time to argue. You want to die, I won't stop you,' he said before

calling out to someone named Horace.

'Find the cleanest bandage cloth you can and wrap this soldier's leg up. Fix some of those thin boards there to keep him from trying to bend it and get him out of here. There's plenty others just waiting for that cot.'

Not even glancing at me again, he just walked over to the next bed.

Well, Horace, a big black man with long fingers and toothy grin on his face, did as he was told. I remarked on his hands because of the gentle way he had in washing out my bloody leg.

'There ain't nothing I can do, boss,' he murmured. Even his voice was soft and tender. 'We ain't got no medicine or nothing that'll help stop infection from settin' in. I's sorry if I hurts you, but ya'll just grit your teeth now.' And I did.

He did what he could to be kind, I guess, in wrapping what was left of my knee and using two long slats to keep it straight. And it did hurt, let me tell you.

It didn't take him long to finish up,

5

though. 'Here's a crutch. I took it off'n that soldier over there. He won't be needing it no more.'

I would have thanked Horace but my leg hurt so much I was afraid to open my mouth. I'd probably start screaming if I did. When I looked up, he'd already gone on to where the doctor was working and had forgotten all about me.

That's when I saw Andrew. I was shuffling out of the hospital tent, trying to use the crutch and not put my hurt leg down but failing at it. What little distance I had gone had left me weak. I stopped to lean against a big old oak tree.

'Cletus? Is that you?' a weak voice, almost a whisper, came calling softly.

I looked around to find who was calling at me and lying there with his back against another of them old oaks was a soldier wearing a long wool frock coat, his head all wrapped up. The covering was bloody in most places and dirty yellow in others. Little of it was

white, if it had ever been white.

'Yeah,' I answered, trying not to move my lips, still feeling like I was going to throw up or scream if I moved anything else. 'Yeah, I'm Cletus. Who're you?'

'Hell's fire, boy. Can't you tell? I'm your almost brother, Andy.'

Now as I might have already said, me'n Andy had joined up at the same time. I hadn't thought about going until Pa died. He hadn't never liked to talk much about the war, said he didn't see any reason for it. I thought I agreed with him, until he wasn't there any more. When Andy came to tell me what he was about to do, I decided there was no reason for me not to go along. Trying to keep things going on the farm wasn't working out. With no other family to help out, our little piece of farm was falling down.

Andy said his folks didn't like it much, his going, but they had already given up trying to tell him what to do. I ain't saying he was as bad as some, but I reckon there was people in that part of

the county was glad to see him go.

Andy's family had lived just down the creek from me'n Pa. There for a time, when we was young, we'd gone to that little school over in town together. That was before the teacher left town. I remember Pa saying something about him running off with the Cranston girl. Why, she wasn't much older than I was, too young to go running off with any man. I was about 15 or so at the time.

When I asked Andy about it, he just smiled and said something like, 'You still got a lot to learn, don't you.' He was always saying things like that. Made me mad. I mean, he was only a year or two older.

Anyway, Andy and me travelled over to LeFleur's Bluff to join up. That fella what put the pen in my hand so I could sign the paper, he argued when I wrote Cletus Cooper. Somehow he thought I was Andy's brother and should have the same last name, Wilkins. Andy laughed over that, but we finally got it straight.

Anyway, both me and Andy put our

mark on that paper and was in the Confederate Army. I don't recall exactly when I learned to read and write, maybe it was that time Pa sent me to school down at Choctaw. But I can. Can do my sum's, too, a little bit, but that don't matter much in this story.

We had joined up just in time to be sent on to Mobile Bay. Andy was a mite peeved to learn when we got to Mobile that most everyone thought the war was about over. There was supposed to be a whole Union regiment: coming down outa Alabama along the eastern shore of Mobile Bay and we was to stop them there. When the shooting started, somehow Andy and I got separated. Now here he was with his head all bandaged up.

'Andy? What the hell happened to you?' Of course I could see something bad had happened and figuring that we was fighting a war, it was clear what had happened. He'd been shot. But I didn't know what else to say.

'I got the biggest headache you ever

saw. That's what happened. What's wrong with your leg?'

'Well, I guess we both was in the wrong place when them Yankees come to call. I wonder, did we win?'

'Naw, it ain't over yet. Listen, hear that shooting over that way?' He tossed a thumb over his shoulder. 'We got our back to the river and no where to go, so the fightin' is still going on. It don't matter none, though. When its all over, I don't think we'll have come out ahead.'

Far off somewhere behind him, I could hear the faint roar of battle. Closer was the screams of men in the hospital tent.

'How bad you hurt?' Talking to him seemed to let me forget for a minute all about my leg and about throwing up. Forget it enough that I started to hunker down so I could talk with him. The stab of pain when my knee wouldn't bend reminded me, though. I closed my eyes against the hurting and leaned back against the tree. Trying to

hold on tight to the throbbing, I didn't hear what Andy said.

' . . . so I don't got to worry about going back up to the line.'

Breathing deep, trying to drag air down into the bottom of my lungs, I focused my thoughts on pushing the pain away.

'What'd you say?' I finally was able to speak. My voice sounded weak and shaky.

'Boy, that leg's bothering you something fierce, ain't it. What I said was, the doctor just shook his head and passed on to the next man when he got to me. Guess I won't be worrying about going back to the shooting. How bad's your leg?'

'I'd say it'll be a while before I can run any. They wanted to amputate but I put up a fight. Horace wrapped some slats to keep it straight, but it does hurt.'

'Joining the war wasn't such a good idea, I figure. What's it been, no more'n a month since we enlisted? Shoulda

stayed home like my pa wanted.'

I let my head droop and closed my eyes. Tired and hurting, I tried to decide whether I really cared about war any more.

'Well, Cletus old boy, I guess we shouldn't just sit here a daydreamin'.'

'What else can we do? I'm not going to do anyone any good back in the fighting. Damn it, I even lost my rifle somewheres back there.'

'No. What I'm thinking about is getting out of here. I'd just about given up when you showed up. My head's still dizzy and there's a roaring in there somewhere that upsets my thinking. But one thing's clear. If those Yanks come through the lines, you and me and every one wearing the uniform of the Confederacy will be taken prisoners. You know what that means, don't you? One of those prisoner of war camps. Not many come away from there alive, I've heard.'

'What else can we do?' It'd always been that way, Andy doing the thinking

and me just following along. He was a lot quicker than me. It was only when he wanted to do something I thought was stupid that I didn't go along, and this sounded like one of those times. 'We certainly can't just walk away. We signed up for the duration of the war, didn't we? They won't let us just walk away. Anyhow, I can't and I doubt if you can either. So what can we do?'

Andy slowly and carefully pushed himself away from the tree he'd been leaning back against. Using the tree to pull himself up, he stood for a few moments letting his head sag. Then little by little he lifted his head until he could look me in the eyes. 'We got to go, Cletus. However we can, we got to go. And I mean now. Come on. If we sorta lean on each other, using that crutch of yours, we can do it.'

Taking small, shuffling steps he made his way over to the tree I was using for support. Putting my arm around his shoulders, with my bad leg on the outside, he nodded.

13

'Now, we'll take it slow and easy, a step at a time. That way,' he pointed with his chin, 'on around the hospital tent. Nobody's going to bother us. They's too busy fighting the battle, looking for help or simply dying. We'll go around the tent.'

Carefully, watchful not to jar his head and keeping my foot from hitting the ground, we made our way. It would have been easier if the ground was level and not covered with rocks and little pieces of tree limb, but we made it. Slowly, we hobbled around the corner of the officer's tent and were instantly out of the stream of traffic. Most of that was men being carried toward the hospital tent. Very little was going in any other direction.

'Now what?' I asked, not stopping.

'Why over there,' he raised his chin once again. 'That big white tent is the General's. I was sent over there to act as a runner for him just before I got shot. We'll go along side it toward the back.'

'There's nothing back there except woods. We won't be able to get through those brambles hobbling along like this.'

'No, but back behind General Liddell's tent is where the regiment's horses are tied. I saw them. They're for runners to use to carry messages back to the fort. If we had horses and went on toward the river, I'd say our chances were real good. Don't go giving up on me now, Cletus. I can't do it alone.'

2

Andy was right. There were a half
dozen or so horses, all saddled and
ready, their reins tied to a rope fixed
between two trees. Some of the saddles
had either a holstered revolver or one of
the newer Spencer carbines in a leather
scabbard. The one I got didn't have
either, but it did have one of the
regulation bedrolls that were part of the
McClellan saddle. Getting to the
animals turned out to be the easy part,
getting Andy up into the saddle wasn't
hard either. The trouble came when I
tried to throw my wounded leg over the
saddle. Horace had wrapped the boards
to keep my knee from bending and
those boards made it nearly impossible.
All the time, as pain made me feel faint,
I kept expecting to have someone catch
us. That only made me move faster,
causing me to bang those damn boards

against everything.

Finally I was in the saddle and with Andy leading the way we left the battle ground. I was almost unconscious from the throbbing and wasn't paying too much attention, my chin was bouncing against my chest.

I don't have any way of knowing how far we rode that afternoon, or even in which direction. It was unlikely that Andy knew which way was home, but, as he did in most things, led the way as if he did. Early on there was times I thought I heard him let out a moan. Mostly he seemed to be riding all loose in the saddle, his head kinda hanging down like maybe he was asleep. Once he mumbled something like he thought his head was gonna burst. My leg was bothering me some though and I ain't sure.

I did most of the ride in some kind of a daze myself, not paying much attention to anything other than staying in the saddle. There were brief periods, I can recall, when crossing a creek or

climbing a steep hill that the horse's scrambling jolted me awake. It was the pain at those times that did it. I can clearly remember the shock of pain. Whether or not I screamed, I don't know. One thing I do know is at the end of the day my throat was raw and raspy.

I didn't know how Andy had got me off the horse, or even how he got through the day himself, but he did. The first time I was totally awake and aware was when I found myself lying on one of the bedrolls with my head pillowed by a saddle. Across the way a small campfire was heating a pan of water. The fire wasn't very big but I could feel the heat of it. Somewhere out of sight behind me I could hear the chomping of horses tearing at grass. Everything else was silence.

With my wounded leg, stiff and unmoving, propped up on another of the saddles, I was almost comfortable. Lying still, I let my eyes close and found that the world wasn't silent after all. Over the beat of my heart and

whatever sounds coming from the animals, I could hear the faint sound of water rushing over rocks and once in a while the call of some bird, but not much else. My heart beat was like a hollow drum, almost more felt than heard. Listening to that steady rhythm, I tried not to think of my knee. Letting my thoughts sneak up on it, wanting to be ready to retreat when I got too close to the smashed bone.

'So, you're back with the living,' Andy called out softly.

Abruptly forgetting my leg, my eyes flew open to find him coming up to the fire, with the wet, shiny blue-black bodies of four or five trout hanging from a slender forked stick. He was smiling like there was nothing wrong with the world at all. He had taken off the bandage around his head and for the first time I could see his wound. Not like my leg, the torn skin on his head was pink and really didn't look bad at all, until he cautiously bent to ease himself to the ground. When he

lowered his head, I saw where a furrow had been cut, leaving a two-finger-wide gouge from the top of his forehead back toward the top of his skull. Bending over, a loose flap of skin flopped down, leaving the gash in plain view, all red and black looking. There was even a bit of grey-white that I thought might have been bone. Water dripped from his hair on both sides, telling me he'd just washed out the wound.

'At least we won't starve,' he said after a minute or two. Everything seemed to be moving slowly. It took a long time for him to get seated. I don't know if it was him moving carefully or it was just the fuzzy feeling I had. Probably a bit of both, I reckoned.

Opening up a folding pocket knife he slit the belly of one of the fish and stripped out the entrails. After brushing off a flat stone that had been propped up facing the fire, he laid the fish out to cook.

'There was a packet of coffee in one of the bedrolls,' he went on to say while

he did the same with the other trout. 'That water's ready to boil. I expect we'll find a bit of chicory mixed in with the coffee but that's the way it should be. Now, tell me, how're you feeling?'

His question caught me unaware. Frowning, I felt like my head was full of cotton as I tried to answer. How am I feeling? Hot and bleary, does that make sense? I realized I hadn't spoken. I had been afraid to move and now found myself scared to speak. How was I? Sweltering like I had too many clothes on and my head didn't seem to be hooked to my body. More like it was floating as I tried to force my eyes to focus. Something was wrong and I couldn't tell him what.

'Here,' I looked up to find him kneeling next to me, holding a steaming cup. I musta dozed off for a little while. 'Take a sip of this. The fish'll be ready in a little bit. You'll likely feel better once you've had something to eat.' Putting a hand behind my head, he lifted me up a little so I could sip the

hot brew. All of a sudden I was terribly thirsty.

'Water,' I croaked. Instantly Andy put the hot cup aside and brought another one, filled with water. I drank it down and waited for more.

'Hey, your neck is burning.' Putting the back of his hand to my cheek, just as Ma used to do, I saw him frown. 'You're on fire, Cletus, and your face is all flushed.'

Quickly he unbuttoned my shirt. He was reaching for the water cup when he stopped and looked toward the horses.

'Damn, Cletus, something's out there.' Scurrying around the fire to where he'd spread out his bedroll, he picked up a rifle and levered a cartridge into the breech. Standing in a crouch, he thumbed back the hammer, his eyes squinting a little as he stared into the trees.

'Come on out in the open or I'm gonna start shooting,' he called, sounding angry and menacing. Lifting the rifle to his shoulder he stopped when a thin, reedy voice answered.

'Do not shoot. We come. We are hungry. We come, do not shoot.'

Whoever it was, was somewhere behind me. Lying on the ground as I was, and feeling as I did, turning to see who was speaking didn't seem important so I just watched Andy.

'You better have your hands empty when you come out,' Andy called. I could see him clearly. His eyes never wavered and his hands were steady, not a tremble showing. The rifle barrel was fixed on something I couldn't see.

'Do not shoot,' the whiney call came again, 'we do not have guns. We are hungry.'

Andy didn't relax, but slowly eased the rifle from his shoulder, keeping it pointed past me.

'Well, I'll be damn,' he said in amazement. 'Cletus, you ain't gonna believe this. It's an old Indian. He looks older than old Grandpa Wilkins even as he was being put in the ground.'

It took me a bit to remember. A strange buzzing seemed to be filling my

23

head. Hazily, I thought about it and then, as if cutting through the fog, I did know who he was talking about. Grandpa Wilkins had been his daddy's pa. He'd died in his sleep when we was a lot younger. Andy was very excited and wasn't very clear with telling about it, but it seemed the old man was just there, not breathing or snoring as was usual.

Scared, he had called his pa who took one look at Grandpa and declared him dead.

'Or, as Pa said, 'passed over',' Andy explained. 'I don't understand that, passed over what?' He had stopped to look to see if I knew, but I didn't.

'Come on closer to the fire so we can get a look at you,' Andy's order cut into my thinking.

I didn't hear anyone coming and when I caught movement to one side, almost jumped. Like a ghost, he moved. Not really lifting his feet, but not dragging them either. Not making a sound. When Andy lifted the rifle barrel

a little, the man stopped. He hadn't looked my way, but from the side I could see enough.

His hair was dirty looking and hung down his back in a long, thick braid. I could see that he was old, his hair was streaked with grey and the skin on his neck was dry and wrinkled. It was dirty, too. I even thought I could smell him, but as woozy as I was feeling it might have been me I smelt. Even I could tell, though, whoever he was, he didn't look like he'd been anywhere near water for a long time. He was wearing buckskin and both his pants and shirt, the tails hanging down almost to his knees, were mostly worn and full of patches. Both garments were streaked with black stains and I could see where in some places the patches had even been patched. His feet were covered by moccasins.

Keeping his head turned toward Andy, he slowly lifted his hands, palms out.

'Nothing,' he said. 'No knife. We got

nothing. Smelled your coffee and came to see.'

I noticed Andy frowning. 'What'd ya mean, 'we',' he asked, then jerked the rifle, pointing it beyond me again. 'Who's that?' he snarled and then called out, 'Come in with your hands empty.'

Again, with no more sound than what a cloud makes crossing the sky another buckskin-clad body floated past me. This time it was a woman, her long grease-streaked deerskin dress swayed as she walked up to stand beside the man. Unlike the man, she stood straight but, like him, I could tell she was old. Like the man, her hair was in braids and looked as oily and dirty.

'Well, I'll be.' Andy muttered, shaking his head slowly side to side. 'What're you doing, sneaking around our camp?'

'Not sneaking,' the man answered, his words sounding toneless and without emotion. 'Smelled coffee. My woman and I have nothing to eat and smelled coffee.'

'I don't think so,' Andy snarled, 'you

know what I think, Cletus? I think they was looking to steal our horses, that's what I think.'

'No,' the man said, lifting his hands in denial, 'not steal anything. Hungry.'

From where I was, just watching and listening, I saw the woman step closer to Andy and peer closely at his head. Holding the rifle up to fend her off, he took a step back and nearly fell over the tree stump.

I blinked and started drifting off but knew I couldn't leave Andy to face these Indians alone. I forced my eyes open and was surprised to find the woman now staring at me. I hadn't see her turn towards me but she did and now all I could see was those black eyes of hers staring at me without blinking. For a long piece of time she just looked at me, studying me from the top of my head down. When she saw my leg all propped up like it was, she grunted and moved closer. Before either Andy or I could react, she was kneeling next to my wounded leg and was gently

removing the bloody piece of bandage.

There wasn't anything clean to wrap my knee with, but Andy had done the best he could, first washing the bloody knee and then wrapping it back up with the linen strip that the black man, Horace, used.

'Hey,' Andy called, startled by her. He started to move to stop her then thought better of it and stayed so he could keep his rifle aimed at the man. 'Get away from him,' he called harshly.

The woman paid him no mind and continued to carefully, tenderly, take the bandage off. The wound, now looking ugly and greenish-black with the dried blood, looked worse than it had when Andy tried to clean it. Getting close, the woman peered at the mess that had been my knee and then, without turning around, jabbered something.

Whatever she said, the old man jumped.

'What's that she said?' Andy asked. I didn't want to take my eyes off the old

woman, but glanced over to see what he was doing. I almost laughed to see him, nervous and not knowing what to do, his rifle barrel pointing first one way and then back. He didn't know what to do. If he came to stop the woman, he couldn't watch the man and if he just watched the man he couldn't keep her from hurting me.

Somehow I didn't think she was going to hurt me.

'Woman says boil water.' The old Indian muttered and without paying any more attention to Andy, crouched down by the fire and grabbed the fire-blackened coffee pot. It had to have burned his hand but he didn't let on. He simply tossed out the rest of the brew and headed toward the creek. When the woman rose up and walked off into the trees, Andy's eyes and his rifle followed her.

All this tired me out and my eyes slowly closed. I wondered if I was dying.

3

I didn't die. Fact is, I'm here today, telling you all about this because of what that Indian woman did that day.

Andy told me later how he didn't know what to do but watch when the old Indian put the coffee pot filled with creek water back on the fire. Not moving, the two men then just stood and stared at each other, not talking or anything. After a short while, Andy said, the woman came back and dropped a handful of bark, moss and what looked like grass stems into the pot. I woke up when she touched me.

It wasn't her putting her hand on my leg that brought me back, it was when she used the long blade of a wood-handled kitchen knife to scrape away the dried blood and green-looking scab from my knee. Andy said I came up like I'd been stabbed with a red hot poker.

He said I didn't whimper, not then, anyhow. I screamed . . . and passed out.

* * *

Sharp like a burst of lightning, I woke up screaming, clutching at my knee. The old Indian woman was sitting next to my leg, holding it down. Across the way I saw Andrew coming up out of his blankets, still holding his rifle and looking for what had woken him up. The old Indian wasn't anywhere around.

'What happened, Cletus?' Andy called, then seeing the woman calmly pressing me back down, took a quick look and, not seeing the old Indian man, let out a curse. Not taking time to pull on his boots, he ran out of the camp and into the trees behind me.

Daylight was just coming on, I noticed as I lay back. That had always been the best part of the day, I thought. Remembering back on the farm, waking up and knowing it was gonna be another long, hot day of working, I

31

liked to lay there and feel the cool morning air brush across my body.

That cool air felt so good, it took me a minute to find I wasn't burning up no more. Frowning, I raised up on my elbows. The fire hadn't been started yet, but everything else was about like it had been. Except for the bundle that was held around my knee by the dirty linen bandage. A big old stub, looking like a moss-covered tree stump, sitting on my leg where my knee was.

'What in Hades is that? What have you done?' I asked, my throat all dry making my words come out in a croak. The woman, still holding my leg to keep it from moving didn't so much as look at me. Before anything could be said or done, the old Indian came rushing through the trees, being pushed by Andy.

'I told you, didn't I, Cletus?' Andy called out sounding happy at being right and shoving the Indian again. 'Told you this was a horse-stealing Injun. That's where he was headed

when you yelled out your warning. Good thing you did, too. He was going for that brown horse of yourn when I stopped him.' Kicking at the old man, Andy tripped him sprawling and pointed the rifle at him to keep him down.

'Damn, I think I should just go ahead and shoot him.'

The woman hadn't moved. Looking at my leg and thinking about how much better I felt, I started to sit up.

'Now Andy, don't go doing something that can't be undone. You sure he was after the horses? I mean he could a got them anytime when we was asleep, couldn't he?'

'Yes, I'm sure. He waited until first light. Hadn't been for you waking up, he'd been gone.'

'Maybe,' I said, trying to think of something to say to stop him from shooting the old man. 'But looky here. This old woman has done something to my leg and I ain't burning up no more. Maybe, just maybe, he wasn't going for

the horses but some more of that moss and stuff she's got packed around my knee. What'd ya think?'

Andy, still standing over the Indian, frowned but didn't let his gaze wander.

'Ah, hell's bells, Cletus,' he said finally. 'Maybe. You do sound more like yourself this morning.' For a long moment he just stared down at the old man who was staring back, blank faced and seemingly not worried.

'Make coffee?' He asked tonelessly, not taking his eyes from Andy, who nodded after a bit.

The coffee had a funny taste to it. I didn't say anything because it was likely from the moss and stuff the woman had boiled in the same pot. She and the old man didn't let the taste bother them. Sitting on the ground, they took turns using the cup Andy handed them and finished drinking it as hot as it was, coming right off the fire.

'We ain't got enough food to share out for all of us, Cletus,' Andy said, talking as if they wasn't just sitting

there. 'There's enough coffee beans left for a couple more pots and that's all. A little salt and a small paper bag of sugar and that's the end of it.'

The woman jabbered something and the old man got up, frowned at her and shambled away toward the creek. I thought Andy'd be after him with the rifle but guess he didn't 'cause the Indian wasn't heading toward the horses.

Nobody said anything, we just sat there, staring into what was left of the morning fire. For the first time since getting shot my knee didn't throb so I felt pretty good. I swear, that man's feet didn't do more than touch the ground. I know I didn't hear him. The old woman did, though. She looked up long before he came back through the trees, holding a stick with a whole mess of trout hanging from it.

The trout Andy had caught and cooked the night before had been split between the four of us and had been right tasty, but I wasn't so sure about

trout two meals in a row.

Well, I was wrong. We had been hungry and when we was done I reckon we coulda all eaten a few more.

I always wondered how it was that dark come on so fast once the sun went down. Especially on a night there weren't no moon lighting up the sky, it seemed to be light one minute and then bang, the sky was full of stars. Well, that's what happened that night. It had been a quiet day, nobody moving around much. The Indians didn't talk, and what Andy and I had to say wasn't much. Now coming on dark, when the fire burned down, I simply rolled up in my blanket and went to sleep.

Hard to say how long that blanket had been on the back of that brown horse. It surely had a strong horse smell, I'll tell you. That was the last thing I thought of. That and a mite happy that my knee wasn't hurting so much.

★   ★   ★

I must have been dreaming about the war, 'cause when I heard the shot it startled me so much I sat right up, ready to run and looking for somewhere to hide.

It was still dark but from what light the stars gave off, I could see where the fire was, and it was out. Across the way, Andy's blanket roll was just a dark spot on the ground. The Indian woman was standing up, staring over at me.

'Damn, I knew it. I told you, didn't I, Cletus?' Andy came stomping past me, holding the rifle in his left hand, a big smile on his face. Even in the weak light, I could see his teeth. 'Didn't I tell you he was a thieving horse thief? He was a sneaky one, all right. But I was watching him. And a good thing I was, I'll tell you.'

Soundlessly, the woman took off running back the way Andy had come.

'Well, he won't be taking any more horses that don't belong to him.'

'What the hell happened?' I asked, trying to make sense outa what he was

going on about.

Before he could say anything, the woman let out a strange keening sound. I'd heard a mountain lion one time. This wasn't like that at all. Whatever had brought it on, it was the most dreadful cry I'd ever heard. Chills chased down my backbone.

'What the hell?' I started to ask, then stopped, thinking about what Andy'd said. 'You shot the old man?'

'I told you, didn't I? You can't trust no Injun. Not when there's a horse you got and he ain't got one.'

'You shot him?' I couldn't seem to stop asking him.

'Yeah. He thought I was sleeping. But I wasn't. I was just waiting. I knew, I just knew, he'd be going for the horses. Hell's bells, there's no reason for them to hang around us no more. They heard me say we ain't got no more food or coffee. Well, I just lay there and waited. When he got up, all quiet and sneaky like, I got my carbine and followed him. There he was, standing there, next to

your brown horse, petting its nose. Getting ready to climb on, I saw. Those Injuns don't need no saddle. Nor bridle, for that matter. They's different from you'n me in that regard.'

'So you shot him.'

'Well, hell yes, I did.'

The woman's wailing had taken on a different sound, more like a long song that didn't have words or anything.

'Boy,' Andy said, levering another cartridge into the carbine's breech, 'that woman sure can make a lot a noise.'

'What do you expect? That old man's probably all she got in the way of family. Of course she's gonna be upset.'

Looking across to see what Andy was doing, I saw how he was just standing there, shoulders back and his chin up a little, still smiling, the white of his teeth almost glowing in the star shine. For a long minute, listening to her weep and moan, all I could do was look at him, waiting for him to move. He didn't.

Disgusted by it all, I turned over, pulling the blanket up around my neck.

Maybe it was the night air, but the blanket didn't smell so bad any more. For a long time I just lay there, listening to the old woman. Somewhere in it all I fell asleep.

It was still dark when I was brought awake again by the sound of a shot. It was almost like I wasn't fully asleep, like maybe I was expecting another gun going off. This time I didn't do more than raise my head to see where Andy was. I couldn't see him. His blanket was still empty.

'It's over,' he called as he came back into the clearing. 'That damn cater-wauling's done with.'

I watched as he leaned the rifle against the tree stump and started getting his blanket unwound. The smile was still, I saw, taking up the bottom of his face.

'You shot the old woman?'

'Now, don't start in on me, Cletus. I tell you, I put up with it long as I could but she just wasn't gonna stop her carrying on. There was nothing else to

do about it. Now go to sleep. We got us some traveling to do come daylight.'

I watched as he rolled away. It wasn't long before he started snoring.

I lay there for the longest time, staring up at what stars I could see through the black of the tree tops. He hadn't always been like this. He was a different Andrew than the one I used to know.

4

Travel we did. For the next two weeks we rode, some days making a few miles and others a lot of miles.

To start off, it wasn't so easy, getting me into the saddle of the brown horse. A fella doesn't know how much a leg does until he can't bend it. Sitting a saddle with one foot in the stirrup and the other sticking out just getting in the way is hard, too. We tried to stretch out the offside stirrup leathers so I could support the leg, but it wasn't long enough. Andy ended up cutting a strip from my blanket and tying a loop. With it hanging from the saddle horn, my leg was riding out there all right. I don't know how he felt, when I asked about his head, he just smiled and nodded.

When we'd gone riding to join the Confederate Army, all we had to do was follow the wagon road from the home

place down to LeFleur's Bluff, the biggest town in the county. Putting a hand on the big black leather-bound bible and swearing to do our damnest was all it took. We was each given a grey wool blanket and a rifle and told to wait with some other old boys.

The rifle was a Sharps carbine. Shorter than the .50-caliber Sharps rifle that buffalo hunters had used. I'd heard somewhere that a good man with one of them could drop a buffalo from nearly a half mile away. The carbine was a lot shorter, a muzzle-loading rifled musket that shot those new metallic cartridges. That was something neither of us had ever seen before. The blankets were simply a long strip of woolen material, wide enough so a man could roll himself up in it. The wool was new enough that if it didn't rain too awfully hard most of the water would just roll off and not soak through.

That was some time ago, though. Now, riding along what trails we could find, we was heading west and maybe a

little north. Andy had taken to riding with his rifle held across his thighs. I don't know what he was watching out for, but he was ready. I just followed along behind always being careful to swing my leg outa the way of things. Some of those trails was narrow. What we was riding was no more'n game trails and I didn't want to bash my leg against some tree or another.

* * *

Whatever that old Indian woman had used in the poultice did it up good. I was pretty troubled that Andy had seen fit to shoot her but all he'd do was smile when I told him that. The poultice lasted a couple days, until the piece of cotton cloth wouldn't hold it together any more. Without that covering my knee, I could see how the wound was faring, once I washed the soggy moss and stuff clean of it. The black and greenish scab was gone and most of the skin around the gash was all

white and wrinkled. It didn't stink so much any more, either.

That doctor back in the hospital tent had simply cut a big hole in my pants leg when he took his look and that's what I was wearing now. Since that day I hadn't had my pants off, or even the leather boot on that foot. I figured when I got a chance I'd have to somehow get all that off so I could get a proper bath. Except for when we had to cross a river or wide creek, I hadn't had a chance to get clean. Back home, Pa made us both go down to the creek every week to take a bath. I don't think it mattered all that much, but he was that way. Now there was some itching going on some days and I reckon a bath wouldn't hurt none.

★　★　★

I was getting pretty good at getting into the saddle and poking my foot in that strip of blanket. Usually we'd ride most of the day, stopping late afternoon or

45

whenever we come on to some water. The coffee had long gone and for food we was mostly eating whatever we could find.

One afternoon, after stopping and starting a little fire, Andy had said for me to sit quiet for a while and he'd be back. I hadn't seen anything, but he had. Later he said he'd noticed a wagon track off to one side and when he rode off that's where he went. I don't know what he found except when he came back he had a big brown chicken hanging from his saddle. The head had been twisted off just like Pa used to do.

Now I gotta say, we cooked that bird over the fire and ate until I thought I'd bust a gut.

'A cup of coffee'd sure be good right about now, wouldn't it, Cletus,' Andy said, after wiping his greasy fingers on his pants leg.

'Andy, you got any idea where we are or where we're going?'

'Well, yes, I think I do. Remember that river we crossed yesterday? I seem

to remember my Pa talking about there being a river that ran north and south with the near bank a lot higher than the other'n. He called it the Tombigbee River. Now we've been riding for about ten days and I figure we gotta be getting right close to home.'

With my belly full, I sat back and thought about that. Home. For me it wasn't much. The cabin Pa and I lived in was a log soddy, built back into a hillside with the front of it squared off with a log wall. The back we'd dug into the hill and the roof was covered with about a foot of dirt. Winter times, whenever it snowed or the north wind blew, it was right snug. In the summer, it was nice and cool inside, too.

The only real structure we had was the barn. It was made of logs, too. Pa's mules didn't care much if the wind blew betwixt the logs. It was dry, and that was the thing. Had to keep the hay we cut dry or it'd rot and make the mules and our cows sick to die.

Andy's home place was a lot more.

His pa had a brother and his family living nearby and had helped them build a real nice log house, one with a shake roof. I'd been in the Wilkins's barn and they'd chinked it up so the wind didn't bother their animal at all. I reckon Pa didn't think that was needful.

There was only me'n Pa to fend for, while over at the Wilkins place there was a whole passel of folks. Andy's ma and pa and a couple younger brothers. Oh, and until he died, there'd been his grandpa. Counting up any nephews or nieces he might have from his uncle's place, well, he could have a whole raft of kin folks to go home to. I expect old Andy was feeling pretty good about being home soon.

We finished off the rest of that chicken the next morning and, after drinking some cold water from a creek, rode on. Finding that chicken was when things started to change. We rode most of that day, coming down off a bunch of low hills until we got to a wide, flat valley. We'd just about started looking

for a place to spend the night when we come up on a well-used wagon road. For a time we sat there, looking at it, trying to decide which way to go. Finally Andy nodded and reined his horse to the right and we stepped out.

The road had seen a lot of travel. Twin ruts, wide enough for each of us to ride in, was parted by a swathe of grass that woulda reached a man's knees if he stood up in it. A lot of wagons had to go by to make it like it was, I figured.

It was just about sundown when we come up to a wide, shallow creek flowing directly across the road. There hadn't been anything to find for our supper, so there weren't any reason to stop. Somewhere beside that creek would do, we thought. At least we'd have water to fill our bellies with.

I'd gotten used to climbing outa the saddle by then, and was just starting to strip the leather off the brown horse when Andy called me to wait a bit. He was still sitting his horse and was

looking off to one side.

'Hey, Cletus, I think there's some light over there,' he pointed the way he'd been looking. It was getting dark enough that any campfire would show up.

'No,' he shook his head when I asked about a fire. 'It don't look like a camp fire at all. Come on, let's ride on a ways.'

He didn't wait for me, but kneed his horse back toward the road. I simply tightened up the cinches on that saddle and swung my stiff leg over it all. I was getting pretty good at that.

As it got darker, the light stood out more'n more. We rode toward it and could soon see it was coming from a house. The dark outlines of other buildings was showing up, too. Keeping the horses at a walk, we rode off the wagon road and into the front yard of the place. For a few minutes, we just sat there and looked.

We hadn't seen any sign of people since leaving those two dead Indians.

Mostly we'd been riding the high ground, away from where we'd likely run into anyone. Andy thought it best, saying he didn't know how someone might feel about a couple of wounded soldiers.

'Hello the house,' he yelled out suddenly, startling both me and the horses.

For a while nothing happened and then a door to one side of the lit window opened.

Moving quickly, a man's shadow came through the door and faded in the dark to one side.

'And who might you be?' came the question from the dark.

'Just a couple travellers, looking for a place to throw down our blankets for the night,' Andy answered.

The man didn't say anything for a long minute. 'Where you coming from?'

'Well, down by Mobile Bay most recently. Left there a week or so ago. Heading for the home place, over near to LeFleur's Bluff.'

'Well, you're riding in the right direction for that. Just the two of you?'

'Yes sir,' Andy was being polite. 'Ain't asking for anything, just a place to bed down for the night. And some directions, if you can help us with 'em.'

Nothing else was said for a time, then the man stepped closer to the light so we could see his arm pointing.

'There's the barn over there. Put your horses in the corral next to it and throw them a bait of hay. You can bed down inside outa any wind that'll blow.'

'Thank you, mister. That's right neighborly of you,' Andy called back, reining his horse around.

We did as the man had said, pulling the gear from the animals before turning them into the corral. Once free of their loads, both horses proceeded to roll in the dirt.

Even with the barn door wide open it was pitch black inside. Before either of us could decide what to do, the man came carrying a lantern.

When he got close enough to see us,

with the kerosene lantern in one hand and the other resting close to a holstered pistol, he stopped and slowly, not missing a thing, looked us over, one at a time.

'Looks like you two've been on the short end of the stick. I noticed your stiff leg,' he said, nodding in my direction, 'and I'd say that fancy haircut isn't from any barber shop.'

Andy had stopped complaining about headaches and I'd noticed where the gash had been was now just a thick scar. It didn't look like any hair was growing back where the bullet had gouged him. If you didn't notice the scar old Andy just looked like he had a funny high forehead. I suppose if he let his dingy brown hair grow long, he could just comb it over and it'd be hid.

'You two wouldn't be coming from the Army, would you?'

'Yes sir, we are.' As usual I let Andy do all the talking. 'We was both wounded over near Fort Blakeley Garrison and sent home.'

'Well, I guess you're just the first that'll be coming along. I been expecting it, ever since hearing the war was over. Men heading back home to try to put their lives back together.'

'What've you heard?' Andy asked, cutting in before I could say anything. 'We've not seen too many people in recent days.'

'Not much. I was in town Saturday and heard that General Lee had surrendered to Grant at Appomattox, over in Virginny. Boys, the South has lost the war. Too bad. Now we got us a lot of Yankee profiteers coming in and disrupting things something terrible. Ah, well. Guess it can only be expected.' Still standing with his hand settled on his pistol, the man hung his head for a minute before looking up at us again.

'I don't suppose you had much of a supper, being on the road and all. I'll go and see what Martha has on the back of the stove. Get yourselves all settled and I'll be back.' The last he said over his

shoulder as he walked back toward the house.

'Well, so the war's over.' I felt dejected saying the words.

'Yeah,' Andy nodded, watching the man's retreating back, 'but we got us a place to sleep and maybe some supper, too. That's the best news we've had in days.'

I was some surprised that he wasn't concerned about the war news. We'd been all fired up to go and help in the War of the Rebellion and now, hearing the South had lost it, all he could think of was supper.

The supper turned out to be a large cast-iron pot of stew and most of a loaf of bread. The man left that with us and bid us good night. We used the last of the bread to sop up the last of the stew. Beef stew it was, full of vegetables and mighty tasty. The bread was fresh and had been baked that morning, most likely.

My first thought when Andy poked me awake was how nice it was waking

up in such a warm, dry, sweet-smelling barn. The dry hay we'd spread out to throw our blankets on had reminded me of the way our old ramshackle barn had smelled. I'd slept good, like a baby.

We was up and had saddled our horses before daylight, Andy wanted to be gone before the man came out. I think he was afraid we'd be asked to do some chores to pay for the supper and place to sleep. Later, thinking about how Andy's hand had not gotten far from his carbine and how the man had kept close to his pistol, I wondered if it wasn't a good thing we skedaddled. I kept thinking about how my saddle partner had dealt with those old Indians, and they weren't pleasant thoughts either, I'll add. Somehow I didn't know this man like I used to when we were boys.

We didn't see anyone as we rode out. I noticed Andy seemed to be sitting his saddle kinda hunched over, his coat all buttoned up. Gawd, I said to my self, almost praying, except I wasn't a

praying kind of man, I sure hope he isn't having one of his headaches. For a while there he'd had some bad ones. Bad enough he couldn't ride and we had to stop while he lay with his blanket over his head, all curled up and still. That'd been right after we left the Spanish Fort area and only happened once or twice. Maybe three times. Since then, he had a couple times said something about having a little head-ache, but nothing bad enough we couldn't keep going.

He didn't say anything this time either, just kept riding. Pretty soon the farm and it's sweet-smelling barn was outa sight behind us. For the next little bit we rode along the wagon road, each of us to a track, and not talking at all. Finally, hearing the rumble of my stomach, I broke the silence.

'Too bad we left so early. Might have gotten some breakfast from him and his Martha. Likely wouldn't have had to work too hard to get it, either.'

Andy looked over at me with a

strange look on his face and broke out laughing. 'Well, we did get us some breakfast and didn't have to work or nothing. Come on, let's find us a place over along the creek.'

I was some shocked at the change in him. Now he was sitting up and smiling a lot.

We'd been riding alongside the creek for some time. The man back there had mentioned that was our best way to go, along the creek until the road forked and then stay to the left. On up a couple more days in that direction. If we come to the Mississippi River we'd certainly know it, and we'd have gone too far.

'What're you so all-fired happy about, Andy?' I had to ask. The change that come over him had been too sudden.

This time his laugh was the loudest I'd heard from him in a long time. 'Come on, I'll show you.'

A little flat piece of ground, big enough to hobble the horses and build

a small fire in a pit served us pretty good. I swung down from the saddle and glanced over to see what he was up to. Smiling like a child at Christmas, he was standing there holding a headless chicken by its feet.

'Where'd you get that?'

'While you was still sleeping I took a look around and found a chicken house out back. Them dumb chickens was sleeping too and didn't even notice me taking one. It was pretty dark and I couldn't tell, but I think I got the plumpest one.'

'Dammit, Andy. That's stealing. And after that farmer fed us supper, too.'

'Yeah, and a good meal it was. But this old hen'll be better than not having any breakfast at all, won't it? And we can use what's left for supper. Here, take it. I got us another surprise,' he said, handing me the chicken. I didn't waste any time and started pulling feathers.

Reaching into both pockets of the coat he was wearing, he brought out his

hands, holding eggs in each one.

'I figured it'd be safe if I only took half a dozen. More'n that and I was afraid I'd have a mess in my pocket. Come on, let's get that fire going.'

It took most of the morning to cook up that hen and there was enough meat on the bird that we had the last of it for breakfast the next day. Those days, from the time we left that farmer's place until we got to LeFleur's Bluff, were about the best of the whole trip.

Andy had taken a piece of rope to replace the strip of blanket and my leg was riding a lot better, and we had more to eat than before. Things didn't start to fall apart until we rode into LeFleur's Bluff.

5

LeFleur's Bluff hadn't really been much of a town, according to Pa. I'd only been there a few times, the last when we joined up to fight the war with the Yankees. Then it'd only been a handful of buildings lined up on either side of a wide dirt street. That'd all changed now.

The first sign we saw riding in of there being a town was a bunch of tents and slab shanties. Further on we could see the buildings of town, but spread out all over the place was these tents. And standing around in bunches was men, most of them I saw were wearing uniforms or at least parts of uniforms, just like Andy'n me. These I figured were from the war, same as us.

'Hey, there, friend,' Andy called out to the first of the soldiers we come up to. 'This here LeFleur's Bluff?'

For a long time the men, there was three or four of them, just stood staring at us, looking us over like.

Finally one of them spit a stream of tobacco out to the side and wiping his mouth with the back of his hand, nodded.

'Yep, it is. Only it ain't the Bluff no more. They done changed the name to Jackson. In honor of old Andrew Jackson, you know.' He grimaced and glanced around at the others then back at us. 'Where you boys coming from?'

'Down Mobile Bay,' Andy answered, settling back in the saddle. 'We was at Fort Blakeley Garrison until we got wounded. Decided to come home about then.'

'Yeah,' another of the men said, kicking at a clod of dirt, 'we all decided to come home, for the good it'll do us.'

'What'd you mean?'

'Look around you. Lots of us, some wounded and some not; most are though. All looking for work or a place to be and none finding it. The war ain't

much more'n over and those damn Yankees are already here, taking over.'

'Are things bad? I kinda figured we'd come to the home place and find things about like we left them.'

One man laughed and the others smiled. 'Nope. Ain't nothing like it was when we left. The Yankees are running most everything and are being proud about it. You watch, before you get well into town, there'll be a blue coat yelling at you about that rifle you got. We ain't allowed to be carrying weapons and they'll be taking it for sure.'

'I don't reckon I'll be giving my rifle to no blue-belly,' Andy growled.

'Then I'd say you better not be riding any farther that way. They's too many of them in town to argue with. They don't come out here to bother with us much. Everybody seems to be just waiting for something. I don't know what.'

'What's everybody gonna do?' I asked. From where I sat I could see maybe a hundred or so men standing

around talking or sitting, staring off at the sky.

'I dunno. We been talking about heading out. Maybe going on west. Somewhere there's got to be something better than just sitting here.'

Andy and I sat there for a long minute, thinking about things. Frowning, he glanced over at me.

'Well, I don't think there's any call for us to go any closer to the Bluff, is there, Cletus? What say we just ride on around this town and head on out to the home place?'

Before I could nod my agreement, one of the men chuckled.

'Y'all from around here?' the most talkative of the group asked and then when we nodded went on, 'Well, don't be surprised what you find. When we say the blue-bellies are taking over, we mean taking over. They call it reconstruction, or something, and what it means is that the Yankee soldiers can do what they want and we can't do nothing back. Not even to protect

ourselves. It's a hard time, boys, a hard time.'

The other men nodded. 'I hear that even the mayor and aldermen over in town were arrested and booted out of the court house. Some army major is now the mayor and he's also the judge. Damn, but it don't leave us anything.'

'That tears it,' Andy said, getting that big smile on his face that he'd wore when thinking about what he was going to do with those old Indians. I didn't like that smile and knew it only meant trouble.

'Come on, Andy. Let's not hang around. We can cut back and circle around. Your pa's place is only a few hours ride west of here. We can be there before dark, we was to leave now.' I didn't wait for him to argue, but nodding to the men we'd been talking with, reined my brown horse around and started back the way we'd just come.

The rest of that ride was in silence. At least between us two. There were

birds flying around and such, just like they weren't aware of the trouble that was clouding up our skies. We rode, Andy in front and my horse staying almost like it was its choice, a couple lengths behind.

Both the Wilkins place and Pa's farm were on the other side of Choctaw, a little village just beyond LeFleur's Bluff. Even now, with all the men coming back from the war, I didn't figure Choctaw would be more than what it'd been. When we lived there, before going off to fight the damn Yankees, that's where we did our schooling. There was a couple of stores, a church, the bank, a stable and no reason for more. Oh, and the empty building where we once went to school. It wasn't much at all, but it served the surrounding farm folks all right, I reckon.

After hearing what had happened to LeFleur's Bluff, both Andy and me thought it'd likely be a good idea to circle around Choctaw, too. So we did.

The farm I'd grown up on was nearest to town and that's where we headed.

I didn't really think there'd be much left, what with nobody to take care of things while I was gone. There wasn't. The roof of the soddy had fallen in and someone had stripped most of the logs off one side of the shed we called a barn. It leaned and would probably fall in during the next storm. We didn't even get out of the saddle, just sat and looked at it for a bit before going on. I didn't even want to go up to where Pa and me had buried Ma or where I had put him in the ground.

All the time we was in the army, I never gave any thought to what I'd do after the war ended. Most of the time we seemed to be waiting for someone to tell us where to go or what to do, and only a little bit was taken up by fighting. Now here we were, riding away from both the army and the only place I'd ever known as home. I thought about it while riding on and figured maybe I'd better be giving some

thought to where I was heading.

Not paying any mind to where we was going, as usual my brown horse just followed Andy's horse. If I'd been riding by myself, I suppose I would have just gone down and followed the creek that flowed past both the Wilkins place and ours. For some reason, Andy didn't go that way. He left the creek bottom and went the long way, up over a steep-sided ridge that overlooked the little valley where the Wilkins place sat. Along the ridgetop he reined in and sat looking down at a group of buildings in the flats below.

'There it is,' he said, low voiced when I came up beside him. 'It don't look like it's changed much. Come on, let's see how the folks are.'

Kicking his horse into a gallop, and letting out a wild yell, he charged down through the sun-browned grasses. I followed somewhat slower behind.

Riding that little bit gave me time to go back to thinking about what I'd do next. Except for being in the army all

68

I'd ever done was help on the farm. Now, with my stiff leg and all, I didn't know just how much good I'd be doing that. It wasn't that I was bothered by it. It was coming back like I'd never really left. Coming back to the same work, same people and same place that I didn't feel good about, especially when there was nobody to come home to.

Andy had his family to take him back. There he was, hurrying down to them while I took my time. I guess I just didn't want to be home, that was it. I just didn't want to go back to what I'd left, just like the war and all had only been like a vacation and now it was time to settle into things again.

Thinking this way, and feeling bad about it, I rode down and come up to where Andy was sitting his horse, talking to a man. Right off, I didn't like the man. The way he stood, looking up at Andy, his thumbs stuck in the wide leather belt that held up his pants, smiling. Not a welcoming smile, the kind of smile a brother or cousin would

69

have. More like a 'what are you going to do about it' kinda smile.

'Now, you just turn those horses around and ride out of here, Reb,' I heard him say as I rode up. 'There ain't nothing here for any of your kind any more. Your family just couldn't pay up the taxes they owed and the place was sold. It don't belong to your people no more.'

'What taxes? Pa always paid the county taxes at harvest time.'

'Now, boy, how would I know about such things? All I can tell you is that Mr Bullock and the sheriff came out to serve the papers. When the man living here couldn't pay the taxes, the place was auctioned off. I stay here to keep the riffraff from taking over.'

'Who's this Mister Bullock?'

'He's the local commissioner. Don't you know nothing? When you rebels lost the war, the federal government sent in their people to take over. Part of their job was to collect any outstanding taxes.' The man chuckled, 'Someone's

got to pay for the war, the war your kind lost. Anyway, that's all I know. It was all done legal like, with Sheriff Pike and his deputies along to keep the peace.'

'Sheriff Pike? Not Amos Pike, for gawd's sake,' Andy said, shaking his head in disbelief.

The Pike family was another of the local families. No one was exactly sure how many kids old Amos and his wife had. There'd been two or three attending the school with us, at least for a while. As I recalled, all the Pike boys were big, not muscle big but more fat big. Round shoulders and fingers that looked like raw sausages. Andy had called one, it was Clarence Pike I think, a pig once and that had ended up in a big fight. Andy said later hitting Piggy Pike was like hitting a slab of bacon . . . all soft, no bones in there at all. The nickname Piggy Pike stuck and that's probably why I wasn't sure if it was Clarence.

The nickname wasn't just because of

his round body, either. All the Pike noses, even the girls', was somehow pushed up so you was looking into their nose holes when you looked at their faces. Their eyes were little beads mostly lost somewhere in the folds of their round pink faces, too. Ugly they were, all of them.

'Naw,' the man shook his head, 'not the old man. He was killed in some kind of accident a few months ago. It was his oldest son, Clarence, what's wearing the sheriff's badge now.'

Andy didn't answer. He just sat there, his shoulders slumped as he listened to the man talk. I saw he wasn't looking at the man, his eyes were slowly sweeping around, taking in the barn and the house. For a long time he looked at the house, a long, low log structure with a wide covered porch that ran the entire length.

'Where'd my family go?' he asked, finally returning his gaze to the man.

The man chuckled. 'Hell, I don't know. They was given time to load up a

wagon or two and told to keep traveling. Most of you Southerners just head west, I suppose. I heard there's a lot of free land over in Texas or up in the Indian Territories. Who cares? Long as they take their slaves with them.'

'My family never had any slaves,' Andy replied angrily. 'Pa didn't believe in them. Not many people did.'

'Ah, the hell with it. I can't spend all day standing here jawing with you Rebs. Just turn around and get the hell away from here. There's nothing here for you any more.'

Coming out of his slouched stance, the smile left his face as the man squared his shoulders, letting his right hand cross over to rest on the butt of his revolver. I hadn't paid it any attention before but now I saw how he was wearing the holstered pistol on his left, with the butt forward at an angle across his flat stomach.

Andy had his carbine resting across his thighs as usual and I half expected him to swing around and shoot the

man. But for a long minute he just sat there, calmly and quietly, before nodding and reining his horse around. He didn't look my way but just rode away, his own back straight and square. I followed.

We didn't ride back up the hill where we'd come down a few minutes before but stayed on the road that lead back down alongside the creek. Nothing was said for a while, until Andy reined his horse to a stop.

'Cletus, I gotta go back. I just got to see if there's anything in the house. You know, like any of the family photos. There used to be Pa and Ma's wedding picture over the fireplace in the parlor. Maybe it's still there.'

I started to follow but he stopped me.

'Naw, I'll go back alone. Why don't you find a place over by the creek there and put on a pot of water. I'll see if maybe there's a little coffee back at the house. I'd sure like a cup of hot coffee, wouldn't you? I'll be back by the time the water's boiling.'

Now I gotta admit, I didn't think to wonder about that gun-toting man giving Andy anything, little enough some coffee. I just did what he'd said and found a place to build a small fire. Seems I always did just what he wanted without thinking about it.

He was right, though. The water had just started to boil when I heard him coming back up the road. I'd been sitting with my back against a tree, thinking about things and not liking it much, and I stood up when I heard his horse so he could see where I was. He was smiling.

'Got the water hot?' he asked, happier than I'd seen him since at least before we had rode into the Bluffs. Swinging down from the saddle, he handed me a cloth sack. Before I pulled the drawstrings, I knew it was coffee. I could smell it.

I put a small handful of the ground up coffee beans in the water and pulled it off the fire to steep.

'Did you find any pictures or

anything?' I asked innocently. Then it came to me, how ridiculous it was for me to think that man would give Andy anything. 'How'd you get that man to give you any coffee?' I asked, fearing his answer.

Andy had hunkered down with his arms resting on his knees, looking into the fire, the smile still on his face. Did I ever tell you that when Andy smiled like that his eyes would have a funny blank look, like he was seeing something far off in the distance. His smile in those times was not much more than his lips being pulled out to the side, showing his clenched teeth. Even so, it was somehow a cold smile.

'Naw, he didn't want to give me the time of day. I had to change his mind.' Smiling up at me, he casually reached across his stomach as if to scratch his belly. That's when I saw the holstered revolver, butt forward on his left hip.

'Andrew — ' I started to say, but stopped.

'Ah, Cletus, you gotta understand. I

couldn't just ride away and leave him there, having kicked me off what had been my own home, now could I?'

Slowly I shook my head.

'It's all right now. We can go on our way, like he said.'

We drank our coffee standing up. After waiting a mite for it to cool down, we stood and sipped, not talking. Looking up toward the sun to get some idea of what time of day it was, I noticed a billowing cloud of smoke coming above the trees back toward the Wilkins farm.

'Andy, did you set fire to the house?'

'There ain't no blue-belly government man gonna enjoy the house my Pa built. Now,' he said, tossing the last of his coffee grounds out, 'let's ride on back towards town. I figure there's one or two things left to take care of.'

6

That's the reason I'm telling you all about this. I don't want anyone to think I came out of the war like Andy did or had anything to do with the kinds of things he was doing. We had joined up for different reasons and I knew that. Me, well, I didn't have any reason not to and I think Andy just wanted to get away from things. To this day I don't know what was going on with him, but I'd heard about a couple fights he'd been in. Pa said those that Andy lost he'd get back at whoever beat him up later, often using a length of pick handle. Fair's fair, I remember Pa saying, and that friend of yourn don't know the meaning of it.

I just want you to know, even then I wasn't anything like Andy. But he was my partner and I couldn't just ride off and leave him.

Well, anyway, we didn't sleep much past sun-up the next morning. Getting close to Choctaw we found a little meadow that was out of sight of everything. We hobbled the horses and hid our saddles and gear in a bush nearby. Andy left his heavy coat behind too, and took only his rifle, and the Colt pistol in its butt-forward holster.

The holster, I had seen, was a military issue. Someone, probably that man back at the Wilkins farm, had cut the flap off and punched a hole for a thin leather thong to fit around the gun's dog-ear hammer.

Not having had anything for supper the night before, except a few cups of coffee, and the same for breakfast, my stomach was starting to growl when we reached Choctaw. It hadn't changed much. Plank boardwalks fronted both sides of the street with a water trough or hitching rail every so often. As a youngster, we used to like to jump in those troughs in the heat of a summer day.

As usual, Andy led the way, staying off the main street and walking behind the handful of stores and buildings. Just near the last building, and keeping close to the alley wall, he walked out to stand so we could see the street in both directions. A ranch wagon stood down the way a piece, the horse stood sleeping on four legs between its shafts. I thought that was in front of the general store.

Looking up the street brought back a lot of memories and I was lost in them when Andy stepped out and onto the boardwalk. With his shoulders back, just like he belonged and had business there, he strode down a couple doors and reached out to one of the closed doors. Naturally, I followed and when he stepped into the dark office I was right behind.

The pair of windows let in enough light so we could see nobody was there.

'Hey, is that you, Sheriff?' someone called from the back. 'What's the chances for some breakfast before you

let me out? Hell's fire, man, I been locked up here with nobody to talk to seems like forever.'

Andy looked around and found a ring of keys hanging on a wall. Opening a door at the back of the room, he disappeared into the darkness. I heard some words but couldn't make out what was said and was just reaching out to pull on that door when it came open and a man I'd never seen before came through. Andy was right behind him.

'This here fella says he's Henry Oskar, Cletus. Says he spent the night in one of them cells back there to sober up.' Andrew was hanging the key ring back on its nail as he introduced the man. 'This here's Cletus, Henry. He's my partner. Now, where do you think the good sheriff will be this time of morning?'

'Howdy, Cletus,' we shook hands. 'I can't rightly say. Usually when I get to drinking too much, he just locks me up until I sober up some. This is a mite early for him to be coming here to the

office, I guess,' he said, looking out at the morning sunshine through one of the dirt-specked windows.

'Well, I guess we can take care of a few other things and come back for him in a while. What say you just skedaddle on outa here, Henry, and go on home.'

'Oh, I'd better wait for the sheriff. He don't like it much when someone doesn't do what he wants them to. I'll just set here and wait for him.'

Andy chuckled and patted the man on the shoulder. 'This time, Henry, I don't think the sheriff's going to care much if you go early. I'll make it good with him, don't worry. By the way, there's a man named Bullock we'd like to talk with. I expect he's got an office somewhere here in town?'

Andy was grinning and showing his mouthful of teeth.

'Well, yes. His office is over there next to the general store,' Henry answered and then hesitated a bit. Looking first long at Andy and then at me, he nodded and went out through

the door. I had the feeling he was running by the time he stepped off the boardwalk.

'Now, Cletus, that sounds like where we went to school, doesn't it?'

Seeing his smile and the way he moved the carbine to his left hand and thumbed the thong off the hammer of his Colt, all I could do was nod.

There were a few more people out on the street now. A tall, tired-looking man was climbing into the seat of the wagon down by the store, and two horsemen came slowly up toward him. As Andy and I crossed over and went back on the boardwalk, I saw the men on the horses nod and touch the brim of their hats at the man on the wagon. None of them looked our way.

Andy didn't stop or say anything about what he was planning. When he got to the door of the old school, he just twisted the knob and walked in. The man behind a wide wood desk was a stockily built man and, dressed as he was, it was clear he was important. He

was sitting with his feet up on the desk, his ankles crossed and his feet in shiny low-topped shoes. He was wearing a dark wool suit. I saw the coat part of the suit hanging from the back of a chair over to one side. A holstered gun hung from a narrow leather belt had been looped over a corner of the chair. Looking at the man, I saw a chain of gold links hung across his waistcoat. His thumbs were hooked in the arm holes of the waistcoat.

He didn't say anything when we came in, like being interrupted was the normal way of things. The other man in the room didn't like it, though. This fella's pants had been tucked into the tops of his boots and his belly hung well over the top of his belt. There was a big pointed silver star sagging one of his shirt pockets. I didn't have to look twice to recognize him.

'Hello, Piggy Pike,' Andy said, his smile only getting bigger. Without looking at me, he reached the carbine he'd been carrying back for me to take.

'What the — ' Pike started to say, his voice loud and gravely. He stopped when the other man said his name.

'Clarence,' he said, waving a hand at the lawman. 'It's all right. I'm sure these gentlemen are here to see me in my capacity of mayor. Isn't that right, boys?'

'Are you Mister Bullock, the government man?' Andy asked, keeping his voice steady and calm. When the man nodded, Andy glanced over where the sheriff had sat back down in his chair. Pike didn't like it and I was sure he was thinking of what he'd do later, after the government man was finished with us.

'Yes, I am. What exactly can I do for you today?' Bullock hadn't even taken his feet off the desk.

'Oh, I just wanted to ask you about the Wilkins place. I'm told you own it now.'

Bullock frowned and started to answer when Pike gave out a yelp.

'I know these men, Mr Bullock. That's Andy Wilkins you're talking to.

The other one, yeah, that's little Cletus.'

Little Cletus? I wonder why he was calling me that. I didn't have a chance to ask though.

'Wilkins?' Bullock asked with some bewilderment, finally putting his feet on the floor and leaning a little forward. It didn't help any, I saw. Andy, still smiling, pulled the Colt and shot the government man right in the chest, driving his body back ass-over-tea-kettle. Pike was slow in getting up and was only half out of his chair when Andy shot him, too.

'Now the blue-bellys'll have to send another of their official crooks to collect the taxes,' Andy said, punching the empties from his revolver and replacing them with new cartridges.

I stood there, waiting, just knowing someone would be coming to find out what had happened and got real nervous when Andy went over and took the gunbelt from the back of the chair.

'Here,' he said, smiling as he held it

out to me. Without thinking, I took it. Andy wasn't finished. Taking the suit coat off the chair, he took a leather wallet from an inside pocket and, without looking into it, shoved it into his pants pocket.

'Well, don't just stand there with your mouth open, wrap that around you and let's get outa here.'

Nobody on the street seemed to have heard the shots, which had sounded loud enough to wake the dead to me, and we simply walked back across the street and down the alley. By the time we got to that little pasture the gunbelt around my waist had settled in and felt almost natural. While we were saddling our horses I asked Andy what he had planned. For sure someone would be coming to hunt for us.

'Well, its likely, I suppose. I think we'll just ride on like we been doing. Head on west and try to find my family, maybe. Now, Cletus, you didn't do any of the shooting back there so there's no reason for you to come along, if you

don't want to. I'd understand if you want to go in another direction. I really would.'

I got to admit I thought about it. Somehow I didn't like the ease with which he had shot those two. And I still remembered what had happened with the Indians. But I couldn't think of anything else to do or anywhere else to go. Anyway, if things got too, well, too bad, I figured I could always ride away.

7

We rode quite a piece that first day or two, putting a lot of room between us and Choctaw, heading west. I don't know if Andy was really planning on hunting for his ma and pa or not, he never said. That first night's camp was a hungry one. All we had was the coffee he'd taken from his home place. In the late morning of the next day we came upon a farm and traded the rest of the coffee to the folks there for a good-sized piece of smoked ham. There was enough for supper that night and the next day's meals.

That night, we made camp in a small grove of pecan trees. There had once been a house and such there but the only thing left now was a stone foundation. Sitting back after frying up slices of that ham and staring into the fire, Andy got to wondering what we'd do

for food once the meat was gone.

'There's a few other expenses, too,' he said, mostly like he was talking to himself. 'It's gonna cost us for the ferry across the Mississippi. I've heard that it's too wide a river to be trying to swim across. Trading that coffee was a good thing, but that's gone now.'

Rolling his body over a bit, he took the leather wallet he'd taken from the mayor back in Choctaw from his hip pocket. Opening it up, he whistled, holding up a thin packet of some kind of paper money.

'Will you looky here. Real Yankee greenbacks. None of that Confederate scrip for that man, no sir. Now we got enough to get us where we want to go. That was our lucky day, old son.'

'Aw, Andy. I clear forgot you taking that. I ain't feeling so good about stealing a man's wallet.'

'Well, what would you have us do, Cletus, toss it into the creek over there? What would we do for money then? We

sure ain't got nothing more to trade off.'

'Well, Andy, we could always stop at a farm or two and see about working a bit. I reckon I could swing a scythe if I had to. It's getting on to haying season. That kind of work would earn us a few meals, at least.'

He snorted his disgust. 'Cletus, I don't know what's coming, but I don't ever want to be farming again. Now learning about cattle or horses would be all right, but plowing or grubbing in the dirt, no sir. Not for me, anyway.'

Folding the money he shoved it back in his hip pocket and then tossed the wallet back into the trees. 'There, does that make you feel better?'

All I could do was shake my head. There was just no reasoning with him.

Nothing more was said about the cash that night. The next day we rode as we had since leaving Choctaw, keeping off any roads or heavily used trails. Riding the back country like that, you don't meet up with many people and

those you do are usually trying to stay outa sight, too.

The first farm we found was easy to circle around and it was still a distance to the next. That's when we ran into trouble. The next bunch of cabins, barns and farms was right close onto a town and from where we sat on a little rise of land we could see the far edge of the town was on the bank of the Mississippi. We had to go right down the middle of the settlement to get to the ferry.

'Guess this is as good a place as any to provision ourselves, don't you think, Cletus? There's no reason for anyone to think we had anything to do with back there. We're just a couple travelling men, back from the war, stocking up. We'll be across on that ferry before anyone even knows we was here.'

That seemed likely and I kneed my brown horse forward.

We came into town at a walk, looking everything over. From one sign telling

where the bank was, we knew we was in Vicksburg. Neither Andy or I knew much about what was further west than Choctaw, except that if you kept riding, sooner or later you'd be in Texas. I suppose that's where we was heading.

We reined over to the building next to a hotel that looked to be a general store. Barrels with shovels and other tools sticking out of them stood on the boardwalk on either side of the wide-open door. Tying up to the hitch rail, I almost smiled when my stomach growled thinking that soon we'd have enough food for a good meal. Coffee with a little chicory in it, too, most likely.

I stopped at the top of the steps up from the street to stretch out the kinks while Andy walked right into the store. Before I could follow, someone stuck a gun in my back.

'Well, looky here. Just like the sheriff figured, if we waited long enough, you two Rebs would come walking right into town. Now, boy, don't you go

moving none. I'm going to take that pistol outa your belt. Don't go looking for help from your friend, either. Old Simmons inside there, like us, he's been waiting for you.'

8

We were dead, I just knew it. Somehow they had found out what we'd done, shooting those men, and now we were going to pay for it. The man with the gun in my back reached around and took my pistol. He had to push me to get me through the open door, my legs just wouldn't move on their own. Planting a hand between my shoulder blades he shoved, almost knocking me to my knees.

It took a little for my eyes to adjust, having been coming out of the late afternoon sunshine like that, but the first thing I saw was Andrew standing there with both his hands high over his head. Men on each side of him had their hand guns pointed square at his chest, one of them was holding two pistols, one was Andy's.

As my eyes got used to the

shadow-darkened room I made out the silver star on that man's shirt pocket. The three or four men I could see were all smiling like we'd been the prize and they'd just come in first and won it.

'I got the other one, Marshal,' the man behind me crowed, taking great pride in it. 'He was just standing there like a bump on a log. Probably part of their plan, one would come in and then the other. Simmons wouldn't be expecting that, I reckon. A plumb easy way to make the hold-up work, wouldn't you say?'

Whatever he was jabbering about didn't make any sense to me, but then my thinking wasn't very clear right then anyhow. All I could think about was what they'd likely do to us. I'd never seen a man hanged before but I'd heard about it and it wasn't something nice to be thinking about. Both Andy and I could only stand there looking at each other, speechless.

'OK boys,' the marshal said, his voice deep and serious like that of Preacher

Armstrong. I remembered one time when me'n Pa had heard that a preacher was coming into Choctaw to hold a bunch of tent meetings. We weren't what you'd call God-fearing people but hearing a fire and brimstone sermon was pretty good entertainment so we rode in to see. That Preacher Armstrong did his job right good, explaining why each of us was sinners and what kind of hell we had to look forward to. His voice had rolled across the crowd, the words strong like they were from God himself. I recalled that tone and it's warning of death and it sounded just like this lawman.

'Which one of you is Wilson?' he asked, looking first at Andy then at me.

'None of us,' Andy said. His voice was quaking and weak sounding.

'Ah, bullshit,' the man on the other side snarled, prodding Andy with his pistol. 'We got you dead to rights and your lying about it isn't gonna help you none.'

'He's right, Reb,' the Marshal agreed.

'You two fits the description almost perfectly. Two rebels just from the war, one named Wilson. You didn't know there was a witness to that shootin' you did back in Choctaw, did you? Commissioner Bullock's secretary was in the next room and heard the whole thing. What you didn't expect, I reckon, was that the federal government would send the law out to find you. Make an example outa you. There's even a reward.' He chuckled, 'I figured you'd be heading west, trying to escape, so I come straight here, the closest ferry across the big river, and I was right. Here you are, riding in like you didn't have a care in the world. Ha.'

Nobody spoke for a bit, then Andy, his face having lost most of it's paleness, took his eyes off me and glanced at the marshal.

'Ain't neither of us named Wilson. That's Cletus there, and I'm Andrew Wilkins and we ain't never heard of nobody called Bullock.' Looking quickly around at the other men, he went on,

his words getting stronger as he talked. 'You're right, we both came out of the war. Both wounded in a battle down near Mobile Bay and we're both heading west. We ain't got kin folk here in Mississippi any more. Cletus's pa died some time ago and mine, well, I'm told they are somewhere over in Texas. The last place we stopped at was LeFleur's Bluff. Heard there about where Pa and the rest had gone. We certainly don't know anything about any shooting, though, not since being shot our own self.'

'LeFleur's Bluff. Guess you wasn't told that's now called Jackson,' the man on Andy's right sneered.

'Well, yes, sir, we was. But it's hard for me to make the change, having grown up there and all,' Andy answered, then looked back toward the marshal. 'We aren't the ones you're looking for. We just happen to be two former soldiers coming from the war, slowly healing from our wounds and going to look for our kin. There's a whole bunch of us soldier boys what'll be coming this way,

I reckon. No reason to be staying where there's no work. We're just two of them. I tell you, Marshal, we is Wilkins, not Wilson.'

'You got any proof of that, boy?'

Andy let his head hang down a minute and then like he'd just been hit by a spark, his head come up and he almost had a smile on his face. 'Why, yes sir. Out in my bedroll, all wrapped up in oil cloth is my family bible. It's got all my family's names in it, up to when Ma died. Pa didn't seem to care to write in any after that.'

'Let's go look,' the marshal said, waving toward the door with his revolver. 'You boys keep an eye on this one,' he nodded at me as he and Andy went by.

I couldn't see the man behind me but the two or three left facing me was scary enough. They weren't smiling any more and they were doing what the marshal told them to, watching that I didn't move. For sure, I thought, they were staring at me so hard I was sure

they could see my empty stomach. It was about then that hunger caused my stomach to growl and gurgle. Nobody noticed and nobody moved. Maybe the growl was from hunger but it coulda been from fright, too. Far as I knew, Andy didn't have no bible in his bedroll. I couldn't think of what these men would do when he came back without the Good Book they'd gone to get.

Waiting for them to come back was hard, especially with them men standing there with their revolvers pointed at me. Standing as I had to, with my weight mostly on my good leg, was tiring. I was sure it was going to give way and I'd collapse, but with all those guns pointing at me I was more afraid to move or even breathe heavy.

The silence in the store didn't help either. For a time there was nothing and then, somewhere toward the back I heard a scratching sound. Nobody else seemed to notice, but I did. Mice, I figured, had probably chewed a hole in

one of the flour sacks that was likely stored back there. The storeowner should be putting out a few traps or getting himself a cat. The thought of a mouse getting caught in a trap almost made me laugh. That's what Andy and I was, a couple of mice caught in a trap.

Scared as I was, I was fighting the urge to smile over that when Andy and the marshal came back into the store. The marshal, I saw right off, had holstered his pistol. Stepping over to Andy, he handed his Colt back.

'Well, boys, it looks like he's right. The family name is Wilkins and his is the last one in there, Andrew Wilkins.' He stopped and then pointed a finger at me, 'What about him? How come his name's not in the book?'

'He ain't really a Wilkins, Marshal. His pa died and we took him in. We was raised together.' The story came off Andy's tongue so easy I almost believed him myself.

'Marshal, you ain't a gonna believe these two, are you?' the same man

who'd been poking at Andy broke in, unhappy with the way things was going. 'They're Rebs, after all. Wouldn't be no big loss if we was to go on thinking they were the killers we thought they were. Nobody'd miss them and it'd do a lot of good, getting rid of a couple more rebels. No telling how many good soldiers of the north they killed.'

'Nope, Aaron, I can't let you do that,' the marshal's voice was still like that of a preacher but now wasn't sounding so hard and stony. 'These boys been wounded. Look at this head and that one there's got a leg what won't bend. No, I think these two have paid for whatever they did. All I'm interested in is finding those two Wilson boys that killed a federal agent and an official lawman. That's all.'

You could tell none of them liked it but they wasn't going to argue with the marshal.

'All right, Marshal. I still think different, though, and if they're looking to make any purchases in my store, well

they can go elsewhere. I won't sell to no mangy Rebs.'

'Now, that's your business, Simmons, just like the law is mine. Sell to these two or not, I don't really care. Of course, I didn't know there was so much cash money floating around that you could turn some away, but then like I say, that's your business.' He turned to Andy, 'You boys were planning on paying for your purchases with cash, weren't you?'

Andy let a little smile curl his lips. 'Yeah, we got a few dollars to pay for what we was wanting.' Glancing over to the storekeeper, he looked back at the marshal. 'Is there another store in this town?'

Simmons didn't waste any time but cut in before the marshal could say anything.

'If it's Yankee money and not any of that worthless Confederate scrip, I guess it'll be OK. You just get what you want.'

The marshal laughed softly, 'You

know, Simmons, that's probably good thinking on your part. There's likely to be a bunch of these boys coming through town and some of them will have some money and need provisioning. Of course, it wouldn't do you any good to be marking up your prices too much for them either. The federal government is working hard at making sure everyone is treated fairly. Boys,' he looked long and hard at each of us before going on, 'here's a little advice for you, too. Get your grub and what not and go get on that ferry. There's a lot of bad feeling here about some things and I wouldn't want you to get in any trouble over it. Simmons, don't be forgetting to give this boy his pistol back.'

Slipping the revolver into the holster on my belt felt funny. I hadn't had it long enough to miss it when they'd taken it from me. I hadn't been carrying the rifle. It was outside on my saddle, hanging from a thong.

Andy sounded almost like nothing

had ever happened. 'That was our plan all along, Marshal. Get on the ferry and head west, get as far away from those hard feelings as we can.'

I let Andy pick out most of what we needed. Not knowing how much of that money he had, I didn't want to get more'n we could pay for. When he was through, we had everything put in a couple tote bags so we could tie them to our saddles. Naturally, I had a hard time getting my leg over the bag but I finally made it.

'That storekeeper said the ferry quits running come dark,' Andy said, reining away toward the river, 'so we'd better get to moving. Likely be a lot safer over on the other side anyway.'

The ferryman charged us a dollar apiece, which I thought was too much. Andy paid it without saying anything, though, so I kept quiet.

We weren't the only ones going west. There was a large canvas-covered wagon pulled by a four-horse team already on the ferry, which was really

just a wide flat raft, when we got there and a smaller wagon came on afterwards. I don't know what the ferry man got for the wagons but it looked to me like a nice little business to have.

I'd never been in a boat before and when the flat ferry left the river bank and started across, it leaned a little against the current. The river was a dirty brown color and, as the ferry was pulled out into the main stream, the water started washing over the upstream side, the side we were standing on. It scared me a little, when that water come onto the boat. I'd never learned to swim and if it tipped over I'd be dead. Almost as important, there was holes in the soles of my boots and I wasn't looking forward to wet feet. I stepped back as far as I could to keep my boots from getting wet.

The trip across seemed to take a long time, but I was too busy worrying about the water washing over and sinking us to pay too much attention. It was kind of a surprise when we slammed into the other bank. For a minute I thought

we'd hit a log or something and was going to drown.

The big covered wagon was the first off and we had to wait. Andy, already in the saddle, glanced back at me and smiled. 'Cletus, this must be our lucky day. You see that man I was talking with?' I hadn't noticed anything but the water pouring over the side of the ferry but I didn't want him to know that.

'No, I wasn't looking, I guess.'

'Well, he's riding with that wagon, there. That's the chuck wagon for a herd of cattle being drove to Texas. It's already gone ahead. He was over in Vicksburg buying up supplies, just like us. Anyway, he thinks there's a good chance we can hire on. His name's Carl and he says we ought to follow along until we meet up with the herd. That'll probably be sometime tomorrow morning. What'd you say?'

'What do we know about cattle, Andy?'

'Not much. That's what I told Carl, that we was farmers before we joined

108

the army. He didn't seem to think that was bad. Said we'd probably have to help with the cooking and not be messing around the cattle at all. Looky here, it's a lot better riding with someone like that than by ourselves. Nobody's going to be looking for two southern soldiers riding with a herd of cattle. We was lucky back there. I'll bet that secretary of Bullock's was hiding under the bed when we was there. He thought he heard 'Wilson' and not Wilkins. I doubt anybody'll be chasing for us long, but it'll be a lot safer if we're with this bunch, don't you see?'

We'd ridden off the ferry and was following at a walk behind the big wagon as we talked. I didn't like the idea. All I wanted to do is ride fast to get away from what had almost happened back there. Thinking about it, though, I could see how it could be better if it weren't just the two of us. Anyway, what vittles we'd bought wouldn't last forever and Andy couldn't be carrying that much more money.

That reminded me to ask about that.

'Andy, how much of that money do you have left? And while I think of it, where did that bible come from? You never said anything about having a family bible before.'

He didn't say anything for a few minutes and then, not looking my way at all, answered. 'Not much. We spent most of it back there. The bible, well, that was our family bible. It had been left in a drawer in the stand by the bed. I guess they forgot it. Before I set the fire, I walked through the house, remembering things. Cletus,' his voice was soft and low as he looked over at me, 'I was close to crying, it hurt so much. We always was a close family. It hurt Ma something awful, my getting into trouble all the time. I just couldn't help myself, it seemed like. Anyhow, all she did was cry when I told them I was going to fight in the war. I hope Ma got over it, but I'll probably never know. Anyway, it was a happy place and now it's gone and I'll likely never be able to

find them. But I got the bible.'

For another long time we just rode along behind that wagon, not talking, both of us thinking about the same kind of things, I guess.

'Anyway, yeah, that bible was Ma's and it has all the names of my family in it. I found it when I took the lantern off the stand there by the bed. That's what I used to start the fire, the coal oil from the lanterns. That's all I took, the bible. And that little bit of coffee.'

I didn't have anything to say about that, so I didn't. After a while, though, I told him I agreed with what he said about joining up with that cattle drive.

'We'll do better if we're riding with someone, especially someone with more food and supplies than we got. So I guess we should see about learning how to do whatever it takes, as long as it takes us to Texas.'

Remembering our run-in with those government men in Choctaw, I wondered if part of my agreeing to join up with the herd wasn't to get Andy away

from having to shoot people. Ever since killing those two old Indians right after riding away from the war, it had seemed to be too easy for him. Almost as if he enjoyed it, and that scared me.

9

We rode steady, staying a bit behind that big wagon for the rest of the day. It was plain that a bunch of cows was ahead of us, the trail they left behind in some places spread out wide. It was going on to sundown when the wagon stopped near a small stand of stunted-looking pine trees.

Andy and I rode up while the man was taking the leathers off his team and hobbling them.

'You boys decided to hire on?' he asked after we'd done the same and thrown our saddles off to one side. He was older, I'd say about the same age as my Pa had been when he died. Short and stumpy, his legs was bowed so I knew he'd been a rider probably most of his life.

'Yeah, if you'll have us,' Andy nodded. 'Seems likely we're going in

113

the same direction and riding alone might not be the best thing to do. You figure there's any Indians or holdup men out here?'

He laughed. 'Wouldn't surprise me. What with the war over, there'll be a lot of young men just like you trying to get as far from all that as they can. They'll have to eat too, you know. As far as getting hired, well, that'll be up to the boss,' he said, taking time to open a wide wooden box under the wagon seat. Tossing a double-bit axe to us, he pointed toward the trees. 'You can earn your keep until then by bringing in enough firewood for supper.'

Chopping firewood was something we both knew about and it didn't take long to have a stack of dry limbs close to where the man had dug a shallow pit and started a fire.

'I'm Carl,' he said, walking back to the wagon and letting down one side. 'I'm the cook for the drive. Come here and help me get things started.'

I'd never seen a wagon like that. The

entire length of sideboards was hinged and when it was opened a couple legs was put in place and it made a work bench. All along that side was boxes and shelves built right into the wagon. Hanging from hooks was different-sized black iron pans and cooking utensils. Carl didn't waste a minute but started taking things down and handing them to me.

'Put this,' a big cast-iron fry pan, 'on a couple of rocks so it's over a corner of the fire. Here, you,' he yelled over to Andy who'd started unrolling his bedding, 'get some water outa that barrel at the back for coffee. You can find a place near the fire to get it heated, too.'

Doing what we were told, it wasn't long before he had supper cooking. Along with the cups of strong, black coffee, he fried thick slices of beef steak. While that was cooking he took three potatoes and stuck them on long sticks then jammed the sticks into the dirt next to the fire to cook. Supper, when

everything was done, was one of the best we'd had in a long time.

All the time he was working at fixing the food, Carl didn't say much, only enough to tell us what to do. I figured after supper, we'd be able to ask him about the drive and the people on it. That didn't happen. As soon as the steaks was cooked he put a big pot of water on to heat. That was for washing the dishes, another job he gave to us. As quick as was possible everything was put back where it all belonged and the side of the chuck wagon had been folded up. Not looking at us or saying anything else, Carl spread out a sheet of canvas for his bedroll, pulled off his boots, climbed in, and in a few minutes started snoring.

'Come on, if you're gonna,' was the yell that woke us up the next morning. The sun hadn't broken over the eastern horizon yet, but you could see where it was getting lighter. Pa always said that sleeping past sun-up was a crime for a farmer. I guess anyone working with

cows thought the same.

Carl already had the fire going and didn't wait for us to help him. Breakfast was pancakes and slices of ham fried in their own drippings. By the time we were done and the coffee had cooled almost enough to drink, the fire was out and everything cleaned up.

'We'll catch up with the herd this morning. They can only move so fast so the cook wagon'll just pass them by and go on. That's the way it works. The herd gets started while I'm cleaning up and then I go ahead to where they'll stop for the night and get supper cooking.'

That was about all he said before using the wagon wheel to climb into the seat. Snapping the long leather reins over the horses back, he was on his way. Like the day before, we followed.

The herd, when we come up to it, was all stretched out in a long line, maybe half a dozen animals wide. Carl kept to one side and slowly went by them.

There was a couple of men on

horseback bringing up the rear and another riding along the side of the herd. They were all swinging the ends of their ropes and, occasionally yelling to keep the cows moving. It didn't look like they was about to stop, being pushed as they were. Up at the front another rider rode along the leaders, keeping them going in the right direction, I figured. Carl, sitting high in the wagon seat, waved a hand at that rider and kept going. A short distance beyond the herd was a string of about twenty or so horses, all tied nose to tail with a rider leading the way.

Carl stopped later in the afternoon close to a small creek. As before, he tossed the axe to me and opened up the wagon side. The fire pit he dug that night was bigger and deeper than before. Andy filled the big coffee pot and put it on the fire. We both stood back and watched as Carl started getting the meal started.

The first rider to come in was a young cowboy, a Mexican, I saw. He'd

been herding the string of horses. I watched as he let them line up along the creek to drink while he strung a rope corral in the grassland off to one side, using a bunch of long iron sticks he'd carried behind his saddle. When the horses were turned into the corral, he walked over to the fire. Without saying anything to anyone, or even looking at Andy or me, he took a cup from the wagon and, using a leather glove to protect his hand, poured himself a cup of coffee.

When the herd got close, the rider at the front started swinging his rope and turned the animals to one side, circling them around. One at a time, like they was used to it, the cows stopped and started munching at the grass. Again, just like the Mexican horse herder, the riders came to the fire, after turning their horses into the corral and, not saying anything, got their cup of coffee. One or two went over to the creek and ducked their heads into the water first.

Carl, working at his workbench, was the first to say anything. 'Boss, I got us a couple riders. They're just back from the war and say they don't know much about cattle but I figure one of them can take Smith's place and the other can help me on the wagon.'

I couldn't tell who he was talking to, the riders all looked about the same to me, just setting like they was too tired to move, sipping at their coffee. Looking around, I noticed that a couple of them were not much older than me or Andy. One of the older ones leaned his head back and rolled it around, loosing his neck muscles. Most of them were leaning back on their bedrolls, legs stretched out in front of them. The Mexican herder had dropped his bedding off a little separate from the others, I saw.

'You boys riding far?' the older man asked, glancing our way after a bit.

'Yes, sir,' Andy nodded. 'Carl says you're going to Texas. I heard that's where my family was headed. Don't know where,

but . . . ' he let his words fade out.

A young man I'd caught looking us over out of the corner of his eye, chuckled. 'Boy, Texas is a helluva big place. You got any idea where your kin was going?'

Before Andy could answer, another youngster cut in. 'Don't matter. What's your names?'

'Andy Wilkins, uh, Andrew Wilkins. And that's Cletus, over there.'

'Well, Andrew, Cletus, the pay is thirty dollars a month but you have to complete the drive. We're heading for the Mason ranch. It's near Toledo, Texas. That is about a month and a half drive, maybe a little less. You make the drive and we'll pay for two months. We lost a hand there in Vicksburg. He decided the work was too hard and took a job in a store.'

This must be the boss of the drive, I figured. A young man from his build, laying back on one elbow, his long legs covered in some kind of buckskin pants. His black shirt was dusty but looked

121

cleaner than most of the others. It fit him loose but I thought he looked somehow slender. He'd tucked the shirt into his pants, the sleeves buttoned at his wrists. A fairly new-looking wide-brimmed hat hung low on his forehead. It was hard to tell in the coming dark, and with his face mostly in shadow, but it looked like he was a square-jawed fella.

'I guess that's all right,' Andy was watching this young man as close as I was.

'Yeah,' I echoed him. 'Seems we're all going the same way, might as well get paid for it while we go.'

'Carl, you take one and the other can start in riding with Freddy on drag. He can take Smith's turn at night-riding starting tonight. Freddy, you show him the ropes. That OK with everybody?'

Nobody answered. From the frown that crossed one face, the young man who had pointed out how big Texas is, I thought he was probably Freddy.

'Cletus, you'll be my helper,' Carl

said, pointing a long sharp kitchen knife at me.

'OK then,' the boss said, leaning back against his bedroll, pulling the brim of his hat down over his eyes.

I was somehow feeling happy to have it over with and having a job. It felt good to have something to do except just riding over each hill we came to. At least for the next couple of months we wouldn't need to be worrying about much. Trying to keep my thoughts to myself, I started laying out my bedroll.

'Hey, Cletus,' Andy whispered and nodded over toward the creek.

Not understanding, I frowned and then saw he wanted me to follow him.

Kneeling by the water, some distance from everyone, he cupped water started washing his face. 'I don't know about this, Cletus,' he said, keeping his voice low. 'Somehow I just don't know if I can do it.'

'What?' I was surprised. 'Can't do what? Ride drag with Freddy? Hell, it

looks like I'm gonna be the gofer for the cook. What'd you got caught in your craw that's upsetting you? If you recall, this was all your idea to begin with.'

'Didn't you see it? The boss. Can't you tell? She's a woman. I can't take no orders from a woman, especially one that's younger than me. She's only a girl, for gawds sake.'

I sat back on my heels. A woman? Thinking about it, I could see that it could be.

'How do'ya know?' I asked.

'I got a look at her when she leaned over. Her shirt don't fit flat on her chest. And take a look at the back of her head, her hair's all up in a bun. My Ma used to put her hair like that when she was working outside in the garden. I don't mind having everybody quiet and everything, but a woman running things. I can't do that, Cletus,' he was almost begging me to understand.

'Hey, Cletus,' I heard Carl yell, 'I'm gonna need more fire wood.'

'I gotta go, Andy,' I said getting to my

feet. 'It don't seem to bother the rest of them, having a woman be boss. I don't think I'll let it bother me none, either.'

'Ah, Cletus,' he said sadly as I walked back toward the fire, 'ah, hell.'

10

That's how I came to be riding with the Skillet crew. I have to tell you, there for a time I wasn't so sure I was gonna make it, either. Carl was a worker, I'll give him that. Up long before the sun ever thought about it, and the last to crawl into his blankets, not counting the night riders, of course, and I had to be up with him.

I expect it was because of my stiff leg that Carl had me take the job of helping him. I didn't ask if that was the way it was. The longer I rode with him the more I noticed that the boss, he said her name was Sally Mason, listened to him when he had something to say.

Miz Mason, he called her, wasn't what I'd call pretty and for the longest while I never did see her smile. Fact is, for the longest time I never did get a good look at her face. It always seemed

to be hid in the shadow of her hat and rarely did she ever take off that hat. Carl explained that days she rode point, at the front of the herd, and didn't have to take her turn riding night guard. No matter if it looked like rain or not, her bedroll was always under the chuck wagon. Carl's was right close by.

Working for Carl wasn't easy. First off, I was to get the fire going in the morning. Then while the coffee was boiling, I'd fill the water barrels if we'd stopped near water and I hadn't got to it the night before. Carl would have breakfast all ready for when the crew got up, and in almost no time they were gone, all saddled and getting the herd moving. That's when we'd clean up the dishes, put out the fire and get moving our own self. Naturally, it was my job to harness up the team, and some cold mornings those horses didn't like it at all.

Stopping where he said we'd spend the night, the work would really begin. Making the fire, taking care of the team

of horses, getting enough wood cut and stacked was most of it until after everyone had eaten. Then it was washing the dishes and taking care of whatever Carl told me to. The big pot of coffee was kept hot as long into the night as possible for the night hawks, as they was called. And then it'd start all over again.

I guess Andy had it just as hard. He'd decided not to quit. I wasn't sure what all Freddy was showing him, but after that first day or so he let me know that he didn't think much of his new saddle partner. They took their turns riding night guard and then spent the daytime keeping the herd moving. The first evening, when they came in after settling the herd down, I almost laughed to see him. Andy had always liked to be clean. Why, he even shaved every day, if he had a razor and some soap. But there he was, dust caking every crease of his shirt. From the look in his eye, I took warning, though, and looked somewhere else.

It was on the third or fourth day that we got to talk a little. He was down at a pond we'd stopped beside, washing up. Someone said it was Sunday and we'd rest up that day, fixing things that got broken and just generally lazing around. That didn't change much for me, though. I still had to fill the water barrels and get firewood.

Andy had his shirt off and was using it to wet the dirt on his chest and arms.

'That damn Freddy is going to make me mad, he ain't careful,' he muttered.

I went on filling the water barrels. 'What's he doing to piss you off?'

'He keeps making little comments about my getting out of the war with all my arms and legs. Not being wounded, he wants to know was I hiding when the battles was being fought. He don't know nothing.'

'Was he in the war? Somehow I can't see him doing anything that wouldn't let him strut around like a banty rooster.' I'd noticed how, when most of the others were tired and satisfied to

nap the few minutes before supper was ready and then head to their blankets soon after, he didn't. Most nights he'd walk out away from the herd and practice his fast draw. He wore a pearl-handled Colt in a tied-down holster and, even when he wasn't using it, liked to keep one hand on it, sorta touching it.

'Well, don't let that Freddy get you mad, Andy. We only got to work with this bunch for a few more weeks. Just don't let him bother you none.'

'Yeah,' was all Andy said.

I didn't give him and Freddy any more thought. That was the day two more men rode into the camp.

* * *

Most all the work set for me by Carl had been taken care of and I'd done what most of the crew had, took a bath in the pond. Other than getting wet when I fell into the water when we was crossing a river a few days before, this

was the first time anyone had had a chance to get cleaned up.

At first, getting into and off that wagon seat was something I had to think about a little, what with my stiff leg and all. Except for the fact I couldn't bend at the knee, I was getting around all right. The more I climbed into and off of that wagon the easier it was. A lot like swinging into the saddle had been.

Andy's head wound was healed up, too. You couldn't hardly see where it had been, unless you knew where to look. No hair grew there, leaving a bald spot.

Andy hadn't been around to talk with me much since he started riding with the crew. Seemed like I was too busy helping Carl and he didn't have much free time, what with riding drag all day and taking his turn at night riding. He hadn't thought my comments about that night riding was so funny when after getting out of my bedroll one night to answer nature's call, I heard

131

him singing as he rode around the bedded-down herd. Carl told me later that was what night riders did, sang softly so the cattle would feel safe and be calm.

Anyhow, Andy was the first thing I thought of when I saw who was standing talking to Carl. It looked to me to be the brother of that old Indian he'd shot back there after we'd left the army. I didn't want any kind of that trouble ever again.

'Hey, Cletus, come on boy,' Carl was all smiles, 'we got us some real meat to eat tonight. This here's Flat Nose George. He's the company hunter and he's brought in the best part of a buffalo hump. It's over there on his pony.' Carl pointed.

I hadn't seen the horses standing hipshot, a huge black load tied to the pack frame on the back of one.

'Bring that load over to the wagon and we'll start cutting the meat up. Boy, we are going to eat good tonight.'

The Indian, after looking me over

from my worn out boots to the top of my head, turned away, not saying anything. Not paying any attention to anyone, he hunkered down on his heels next to the fire pit, reaching out for the blackened coffee pot that sat on a rock keeping hot.

We'd eaten up all the meat Carl had bought back in Vicksburg and had even had to kill one of the older cows from the herd. Feeding this many hard-working riders took a lot of food.

'I counted on Old Flat Nose coming in a couple days ago,' Carl said as he sharpened his thin-bladed knife on a whetstone. 'Usually he brings in something about every second day or so. Sometimes a deer or antelope, and even at times a passel of prairie chickens. I guess getting this buffalo took him a mite longer than usual.'

Carl was good with that knife, cutting thick steaks off and piling them to one side.

'Boy, you make sure we got us a good bed of coals there in the pit and then

get that wire grill off from under the flour and set it about a foot or so above 'em. Once the boys see what we got cooking, they'll be all over us for supper.'

He was right. Nobody paid the Indian any notice, but once one of the riders saw the meat on the fire, the word spread fast. Before Carl had turned the first steak over to cook the other side, most all were standing close by, tin plate in hand, waiting their turn.

This was the first buffalo I'd ever had and didn't know what to expect. Let me tell you, it is different from beef. When I sopped up the last of the juice with a biscuit left over from breakfast, I was already thinking about the next day's supper.

Carl didn't say anything, so I didn't make any sudden moves to get the water heating for washing up, sorta sat and let the meal settle. But it had to get done before dark, so I got busy. I had my arms elbow deep in the tub we used to wash dishes in when I heard a horse

coming in to camp.

Mostly the herd had been circled on the other side of the pond and whoever was riding guard had already started their endless circling and singing. The horse herd, Carl called it the *remuda*, had been watered and turned out in the rope corral Juan Gomez had set up. The rider I heard approaching was coming from the other side of things.

'Hello, the camp,' a man called from somewhere on the other side of the wagon from me. Carl had been talking with the boss and turned to see who the newcomer was. I saw him say something to Miz Mason and then walk out of my view. The Indian also stood up and walked the other way, over to where he'd left his horses.

Flat Nose George had two horses, one was a dirty brown and white pinto and the other was really a commonplace mule. Both looked tired and scruffy. Even now, a good two or three hours after being off saddled, they looked beat. George pushed one away

from the pile of saddle, pack frame and bedroll and slipped the bit into the mouth of the other. After swinging his saddle on to the back of the pinto and cinching it up, without looking at anyone, he climbed aboard and, leading the mule, rode out into the night's darkness.

Finishing up, I threw the soapy wash water out of the tub and hung it from its peg on the wagon. Wiping my hands dry, I looked over to see a tall, broad-shouldered man step into the fire light. From his wool suit coat and matching dark pants, I didn't figure this to be someone riding the grub line. We'd had a couple of those kind, men riding in looking for work and, if it was near meal time, staying around to eat before riding on. Carl said he reckoned there'd be a lot of them in the next few months, men looking for work.

This fella wasn't like that. This one looked like he might even be a ranch owner. He stepped over and shook Miz Mason's hand and then stood next to

her, talking softly. Carl came out of the dark and hunkered down next to the fire, poking at it with a stick. Nobody looked my way as I went over to where I'd left my bedding. With a full stomach, and remembering how good it had all tasted, I didn't have any trouble falling asleep.

Before closing my eyes I watched the stranger standing by the fire. He stood there talking to Miz Mason, his shoulders squared off just like some of those officers I'd seen back at Fort Blakeley Garrison. The coat he was wearing wasn't like any officer's coat I ever saw, though. This fella's coat was of a fine cloth, it looked. What you'd figure a banker would wear, not someone out riding for no reason. Maybe I was being dumb like a kid, but I had taken a dislike of him. Whatever the reason, I fell asleep not thinking good thoughts about the newcomer.

Carl told me a little about Capt. Sterling Holden the next day.

The Captain, according to Carl, was

a mustered-out Confederate officer who'd been wounded at the Battle of Sabine Crossroads and discharged. Miz Mason had hired him back in Vicksburg to guide the herd across and into Texas. He'd come pretty highly recommended, Carl said, by a fella that said he knew Miz Mason's pa.

Holden had gone on ahead and only caught up with us now because he'd been checking on waterholes, creeks and the like, finding the best way to go. That was about all the cook said about the man but somehow I got the feeling that he didn't think much of the former army officer, either. Thinking back to Flat Nose George's quick departure, I wondered about it all.

11

The cattle drive took on a sameness that was hard to put up with, almost like back when me and Pa was plowing, doing the same thing every day, sun-up to sun-down. Working for Carl, early in the morning I'd do up the pots and pans that he had used to cook breakfast. Then, if we was near a stream or pond, fill the water barrels. Carl would be busy doing whatever it was he did, and then one or the other of us would harness up the team and we'd be off. The rest of the day was spent passing up the herd, which had got its start before the sun was up, until we found where we'd stop for the night. Carl would get the supper fixings ready while I dug the fire pit and gathered firewood and, well, just made myself useful. After supper was done, I'd clean up and by that time it was late and the

day had been long.

The next morning, whoever was riding night patrol would wake us up and it'd start all over again.

The country we was going through wasn't much different from what we had back home. Mostly rolling hills all covered with wild grasses, bunches of low-growing brush. Carl said it'd probably make good cattle-raising land, but nowhere near as good as over in Texas.

'Boy, you'll like Texas,' Carl said one morning. The older man hadn't been too talkative and I didn't want to intrude so hadn't asked many questions. Maybe he just had to get to know me, I don't know, but this one morning he wanted to talk, and from then on, he did.

'Texas country is big. It's got all kinds of room for a man to grow in. The land's a lot like this, wide and open, clear to the horizon. Not many people living out anywhere near the Skillet, and that's good. The nearest town, Toledo, isn't much, but it's got

everything the ranchers in that part of the state need. You'll like it, if you and your partner is thinking of staying around.'

He didn't go on for a while and I think he was waiting for me to tell him about me'n Andy. I thought about it for a bit and then told him about Andy looking for his family.

'His pa lost their farm to a crooked sheriff and some Union government man. Someone told us what was left of his family loaded up a wagon and headed west into Texas.'

Carl thought about that a while. 'What'd you say the family name was?'

'Wilkins,' was all I offered.

'Now that does sound familiar,' he said. 'I seem to recall hearing about a number of wagons filled with families getting shut of the war and moving into the Fort Worth country. That'd be further west of the Skillet. Probably that's where you'll find your family.'

I didn't say anything and let him think Andy and me was kin folk.

For a long stretch he didn't say anything, and I thought he was finished talking. But he wasn't.

'They're calling it Reconstruction, them Union men,' he said, almost like he was talking to himself. 'As fast as the surrendering papers were signed they come in, officials with orders to make sure every business and ranch or farm kept producing. That way the Union government could collect the taxes. I read in a newspaper back there in Vicksburg that all the taxes paid in the South was to pay off the debts of the northern states. A lot of people, just like yours I guess, are just packing up and heading farther west. GTT, they're calling it, Gone To Texas.'

I didn't know anything about that, so couldn't comment.

It was like that for the next few days. We'd be sitting there, watching the tail ends of those horses, pulling us on toward evening time. Once in a while he'd say something about Texas, or the Mason family.

'I was with old Alexander Mason back in Pine Bluff, you know,' he'd start out, and then talk a bit about whatever he'd been thinking about. 'When it looked like there was going to be a fight with those government people up in Congress, the old man said he didn't want any part of it, so he sold out. He kept a good-sized bunch of his best cows and horses and we pushed them down into Texas.

'That was a trip, let me tell you. Alexander wasn't exactly sure where we was going, just that he'd heard about land being available for settling there, down in the Red River country. Sally was a young one and mostly rode with her mother in a wagon. Even then she really wanted to be in the saddle and work along with the crew. That was just me and Homer and a couple of other boys we picked up to help out.' Carl chuckled softly. 'That's how Alexander named the new ranch, you know. He'd say, 'Boy, it's likely we're jumping right out of the frying pan and into the fire.'

143

And when we got to Texas and it came time to register the brand, that's what he made it, a circle with a handle, a frying pan. Only he called it a skillet.'

Taking about it had clearly brought back memories for the man. He stopped talking for a while, just sat and remembered those days before going on.

We'd been feeding the crew and I'd been washing up their dirty dishes for some time, but I didn't know much about any of them. I didn't know which one was Homer Pickins, but I knew who Juan Gomez was. He was a little younger than me, I figured. We'd talked a bit when I was turning the team out into the corral he'd set up each evening. I was even picking up a few words of Mexican from him.

It was Freddy Juarez I asked about next.

'Freddy?' he looked at me from the corner of his eye when I asked. 'Well, he's about your age, I'd say. He thinks he's too good to ever work for the camp

cook. Any work that can't be done on the back of a horse isn't fitting work for a man, he's sure to say.'

Carl chuckled. 'Of course, a man's got to have his pride. But some seem to have a bit too much, I think. The way he's always working his holster, or cleaning that Colt he bought. He seems to spend a lot of time practising drawing his pistol. It's likely he thinks he's fast at getting that Colt out of leather.'

Carl stopped talking and sat, his shoulders slumped and the reins held loosely in his gloved hands. 'A pistol like that is only a tool. It isn't some kind of plaything. I reckon it takes a lot more to pull a gun and shoot someone than just being fast. He hasn't learned that yet and it's likely it'll be too late when he does.'

I didn't want to talk about that. It made me wonder more about someone who seemed to like shooting people and I didn't even want to think about that. Anyway, the one person I waited for

him to talk about never came up. Somehow the talk never got around to Miz Mason.

★   ★   ★

Flat Nose George came into camp more frequently after that first time when he'd brought in the buffalo. He'd come in with a deer carcass tied across the back of the mule, or a couple of antelope, stay the night and ride out again after breakfast.

Capt. Holden spent one or two days before riding out again. Mostly during those days he was riding at the front of the herd alongside Miz Mason. I'd see them as we pulled past, the square-shouldered man waving his arms as he told the young woman something. Probably telling her about where the herd would find the best travelling, I figured. That doesn't mean I liked it, him being so friendly with the boss. Carl didn't like it either.

'You keep an eye on that fella

whenever he's around the camp, Cletus,' was all he said that morning.

Later in the afternoon, as we was riding along, with me jumping off the wagon at one point or another to pick up some of the dry wood Carl had seen, that Indian, Flat Nose George, came riding up. I gotta admit, I'd been dozing at just that moment and hadn't even noticed the small stand of pine trees we was passing. While I was using the big axe to chop up some tree limbs, I glanced over to see the two men talking.

George didn't stick around long and was gone by the time I had cut up all I could. Carl helped me load the chunks into the wagon and we was soon on our way again.

For a while nothing much was said, then Carl told me what the Indian hunter had told him.

'Seems our tame Indian has spotted the good Captain Holden a lot lately,' Carl said. You could tell he liked hearing bad things about the man

who'd been hired to guide us. 'George says he's spotted Holden talking with a couple riders twice the last few days. The men were strangers to George, and he was careful not to be seen by any of them. Wonder what it means.'

Well, probably nothing, was my thought but I didn't say anything. It was true, there just weren't that many men to be seen riding around out here on the plains, but then again, that's about what it'd have to be.

Old Flat Nose George wasn't a bad man, I'd discovered. It had worried me a mite when he'd come up on me once when I was checking on some of my gear. Everything I owned had all been stashed in the back of the wagon under a couple sacks of flour. Those sacks were about empty and I had wanted to see how my things was doing. There wasn't much: that army saddle, the rifle Andy had given me and the revolver he'd taken off that government man he'd shot back to Choctaw.

I had the rifle in my hands and had

just levered the breech open to make sure it was empty when the hunter came up beside me.

'Good rifle,' he muttered and reached out to take it from me. I didn't like that, but before I could react, he had levered a shell into the breech and shoved it back in my hands. 'Gun no good if not loaded,' he said and nodded abruptly before turning to walk away.

I thought about it a minute and had to agree. With the safety on it was not going to be causing any trouble, and you just never knew.

That was the only time he had ever talked to me, but it was enough for me to feel that he was a good man to have around.

As the days went by, things on the drive didn't change a great deal. There wasn't time for me'n Andy to talk about things, much more'n asking how's it going. Whether it was keeping the herd together and moving along steadily or feeding the crew, there just wasn't a lot of spare time.

What I could see, though, was things hadn't got any better between him and Freddy Juarez. You could tell from the way they were so careful not to get too close to each other. I'd see them at any meal, one sitting on that side of the fire and the other over on the other side, not looking at each other or anything.

Most of the others would joke a little, or talk quietly about this or that, but not them two. No, sir, it was pretty clear they didn't like each other much.

That was the way it went, everybody doing his job and staying out of the other's way. Until we got near a little town called Farmerville, that is. Then things changed.

12

'Boys,' Miz Mason said one night about the time everyone was finishing up their supper. 'Boys, we're making pretty good time and are about where we planned on being, but our food supplies are going down faster than I expected.' She stopped for a minute, looking around to make sure everyone was listening. Even, I saw, Capt. Holden. He was standing off to one side, almost outside the light from the campfire.

'Now, Captain Holden here, says we're just about a days drive to a small town named Farmerville. A general store there'll have everything we'll need to get us to the next big town, which is Shreveport. Just past Shreveport is where we turn north and cross over into Texas. It's only another week or so after that and we'll be on ranch property.'

That got some of the men to talking.

The end of the drive was almost in sight.

'However,' she went on, raising her voice to get everybody's attention again, 'there's still the need for Carl to go do some shopping. To be fair about it, I think we've been on the road long enough without a break, so we'll find our campsite tomorrow evening and set up for two days. That'll give everyone at least one day and night in town.'

Now she really had everyone's attention. For the first time in I couldn't think of how long, there was real laughter in camp. Not that it'd been an unhappy camp, but it had always been a camp full of hard-working, tired men. With the thought of spending some time in a town, that tiredness was forgotten.

That feeling was still there in the morning, with the men jostling with each other as they saddled up for the day's work. All in good fun, you understand.

There surely didn't look like there

was any town near the place Carl chose to stop in later that day. When I commented on it, he just laughed and used a thumb to point at a small rise just a bit further on.

'Go take a look from up there, boy.'

It didn't take me much to climb up there, and he was right, there was a little flat valley on the other side. Somewhere off there, about a mile or so, I'd guess, was the town. Miz Mason had said it wasn't much and that was for sure. No more than a half dozen or so single-storey buildings, from what I could see, all wood and some with false fronts. Somehow it reminded me of Choctaw, back home.

'You and me,' Carl said, smiling at me, 'we can go in as soon Juan brings up the remuda and we get our hair combed. We'll take a couple horses to pack what supplies we can get. You do remember how to ride a horse, don't you?' It'd been a long time since he'd done any joking around.

It didn't take us long to get saddled

up. I noticed that Carl had changed his shirt, too. I only had the one I was wearing, so there wasn't much I could do about that. We were out and away from camp before the herd was brought in and circled for the night.

Farmerville wasn't as much of a town as Choctaw was, I saw, riding in a short time later. Carl headed straight for the biggest building, the one with a sign reading General Store & Saloon over the front. The door to the store was just a regular door but the saloon doors, on down the walkway a bit, was different. Those was two doors, facing each other and cut in half. The bottom halves was closed, the top half open like a window onto the street. I'd never seen anything like that before.

Carl took his time looking at what was on the shelves of the store, asking the shopkeeper about prices of things. There didn't look to me to be much there, but when we had our two packhorses loaded up, there was a lot less. While we'd been inside making our

purchases, most of the rest of the crew had ridden in.

'Now, Cletus,' the cook said, standing by his horse, 'I'm gonna head back to the wagon and unpack this stuff. I'll wait until tomorrow to come in and wet my whistle. You can do what you want, come on back with me or go on to see what the town has to offer.'

I didn't have any money, so thought I'd ride back with him. That was when Andy stuck his head out the saloon door and called to me.

'Hey, partner, come on in and I'll buy you a glass of beer.'

Well, that settled it. Nodding to Carl, I headed into the half doors.

Both the store and the saloon had windows on each side of the doors, but somehow the store was better lit. I stopped just inside the saloon to let my eyes adjust. I hadn't been in that many saloons in my life so didn't know exactly what to expect. There wasn't much, let me tell you. A couple wood planks had been set on barrels with the

customers standing on one side and the bartender on the other. About half way down I saw Andy waving at me.

'Don't forget,' Andy leaned over to whisper in my ear, 'I've still got that cash money we took from that fella who called himself the mayor.' Then standing away, he laughed. 'We ain't got much but enough to pay for a beer or two and maybe even go over to get us a new shirt. I'm getting tired of wearing these army clothes.'

You got to hand it to them, though, the pants and shirts they'd given us when we joined the army had worn pretty good. Yeah, they was getting a mite threadbare in spots, but for all that we was still covered up decently. New pants would be nice, though.

'What,' a loud voice down the plank bar hollered out, 'you fella's too good for the clothes the Confederate Army gave you?'

Andy glanced over his shoulder and smiled. 'Well, no, can't say that. After all the time we've been wearing them,

back there fighting at the Battle at Spanish Fort and all, I guess they've earned their rest. What battles did you fight in, Freddy?'

Slowly, taking their beer glasses with them, all the men standing between the two men stepped back out of the way. Nobody was talking or laughing any more.

'You know my Pa wouldn't let me join up,' Freddy Juarez snarled, standing away from the bar, facing Andy. 'But that don't mean I'm gonna stand here and let you or anyone down-talk the Confederacy.'

'Boy,' Andy's voice got quiet and soft and without looking I knew his smile was cold, 'I did my fighting for the South so I reckon I can say nearly anything I want. Now, if you don't like it, that's all right, too.' Pushing himself from the bar, he turned and put his back to the planks. 'Cletus,' he said not looking away from Freddy, 'you mind stepping over there a bit?'

Quickly I joined the others leaving

the two men alone. Even the bartender had moved away.

'Now, Freddy, you've been ragging me since I hired on. Why is that, I wonder?'

'I'll tell you why.' Freddy was standing with his shoulders kinda hunched forward, his arms hanging loose at his sides, right elbow bent a little so his hand was close to his pistol butt. 'You came in there with your head wound, acting all so mighty, being a wounded soldier. Making yourself out to be a big deal, and everybody making over you 'cause you was wounded in a battle. But you didn't know so much. I even had to teach you what riding drag meant. And all the time you thinking you're so much better than the rest of us.'

As he spoke, the words coming out, spraying spittle with each one, his upper body crouched even more. From where I stood I could see Andy's face and I was right, his smile was the same as I'd seen before, cold and thin.

Shaking his head a little, he started to turn away. Someone, I don't know who, started to say something, maybe give a warning, when Freddy's hand came up, his fingers closing around the butt of his pistol. I was watching Andy. He had just begun to turn away, letting his hand cross over his stomach, when he pulled his Colt free from the leather and shot Freddy.

The young cowboy staggered back a real surprised look on his face and dropped his half-drawn pistol as he clutched at his stomach. Andy, his lips pulled back in a stiff grin, shot him twice more.

13

Nobody moved for a long minute and then, as if someone opened the gate, everyone was talking at once, telling each other what had happened.

Andy didn't pay any attention to anyone, just shoved his revolver into the holster and stepped back to the bar. He was taking a big swallow of beer when the half-doors swung open and a big-bellied man came pushing in.

'What the tarnation was all that shooting?' he called out, stopping just inside to look around. Seeing unfamiliar faces, he squared his round shoulders and let the smile fall from his face. I was watching and saw how big and round his eyes got when he saw Freddy lying flat out on the floor.

'Will someone tell me what's that all about?' he said, straightening his waistcoat so we could see the silver star

pinned above the pocket. 'Who are all you boys and which one of you shot that fella?'

At once, four or five people started telling the sheriff what had happened. With everyone talking at once, none of it made any sense. Finally, holding up a hand to stop the talk, he pointed at the bartender.

'Harry, you tell me, what this is all about,' and Harry did. When the bartender pointed toward Andy, I stepped back without even thinking, leaving him by himself, leaning against the bar with a glass of beer in his hand.

'It was as fair a fight as you could ask for, Sheriff,' someone called from the side of the room.

'Well, Amos, I can see that. The dead fella's pistol is right there on the floor next to his hand.' Stepping over, he stood looking down at Freddy for a minute then around the room.

'All right. This was a fair fight, as has been pointed out. Seeing as how none of the principals involved are town

people, then I guess it's not a matter for the judge. However, this is a friendly town, one that welcomes people coming in, especially if they're here to buy supplies like I been told you did. What I'm going to decide is not to worry this any further. You take your dead rider with you and once you've got everything you need, keep riding.'

Standing there like he was, his feet planted somewhat apart and his one hand firmly on the butt of his holstered revolver, he didn't look so round and soft as he did earlier. The stern look on his face left his order for us to leave town with no room to argue. Andy hadn't even turned around. He calmly finished his glass of beer and, not even glancing at where Freddy lay, walked out the door.

I frowned. On one hand, he had clearly enjoyed shooting Freddy and that troubled me. On the other, it was almost funny the way he didn't seem to be bothered by the killing. Maybe, I thought as I drained my beer glass, it

really wasn't so funny after all. That was the same way he'd looked to feel about shooting those Indians and the men in Choctaw. A lot like it didn't bother him at all.'

I was still frowning as I pushed outside to stand on the boardwalk, watching my partner ride calmly down the street and out of town. Wasn't that show of no feelings what had bothered me and made me glad to be riding on the wagon with Carl?

* * *

Homer and a couple of the other hands tied Freddy's body onto the back of his horse and brought it back to camp. By the time we all arrived, somber and silent, Andy had already unsaddled his horse and was rolled in his blankets. After quietly explaining what had happened, someone dug a shallow hole off a ways and Freddy's blanket-wrapped body was buried. Miz Mason stood at the head of the grave and read

a few words from a bible. I didn't even know there had been one in camp.

Nobody said much. Well, a couple of the riders who hadn't gone into town cussed when they heard that we weren't wanted in there any more, but that was about all. Carl refilled the big coffee pot and those who didn't pull off their boots and crawl into their bedroll sat around and sipped the hot brew.

'That'll make us one hand short on the drive,' someone said.

'Carl,' Miz Mason asked, 'were you able to get everything you need to keep us fed until we get to Shreveport?'

'Yes ma'am. There wasn't a whole lot there, but I was able to get enough. We might have to make do on a few things if we're not there in four or five days.'

'Good. I suppose the best thing to do is have your helper take Freddy's place on drag.' I had been half asleep and only half listening when it came to me I was the one she was talking about.

'Me?' I said stupidly, coming full awake.

'Yeah. Didn't you have a saddle when you came into camp?'

'Well, yeah. One that was on the army horse we, uh, was given when we left the army.'

Carl laughed softly. 'You know, it seems that I heard somewhere that when the war was over, each soldier was given a horse to ride home on. The officers got to keep their weapons.'

'Miz Mason?' Homer, sitting with his back to a wagon wheel, called out quietly, 'those army saddles aren't no good for working cattle. There's no horn on them, no place to tie off your lasso if you have to. We had that old one in the wagon what we gave to young Andy there. I'd suggest that if you're gonna have Cletus ride drag, he take Freddy's hulk. For certain, he ain't gonna use it no more.'

Nobody said anything for a while. Slowly, one by one as they finished their coffee, the riders dropped their cups into the washtub and found their blankets. Finally, only me and Miz

Mason was left sitting by the fire. I couldn't think of anything to say and didn't feel comfortable being kinda alone with her, so I got rid of my cup and, muttering something like 'Good night' unrolled my blankets.

I hadn't noticed Andy laying close by.

'Guess it's you and me again, Cletus,' he said, keeping his voice down so as not to disturb anyone. 'It ain't hard work. I can show you real quick.'

I wanted to talk to him about the shooting and ask why he'd shot Freddy those extra times, but didn't. Maybe when we was riding I could find out what was bothering me.

'Yeah, I guess,' was all I could say. Once again, I was sure of being painted with the same brush and I didn't know what to do about it.

* * *

Riding drag, as Andy said, wasn't hard, but it was work. I'd never noticed before, but the dust kicked up by all

those hooves was terrible. Even with my threadbare neckerchief tied up around my mouth and nose, it was hard to breathe at times.

Keeping the cattle moving was the main thing, but making sure none of them wandered off was what kept us busy. There was no time to sit and talk. You'd think after being pushed along for as many days as they were the cows would know to stay with the herd. Not these stupid animals. It was the young ones causing the most trouble, every so often one or another would decide to go after a clump of grass off to one side or the other.

Mostly, though, the herd just moved along at a walk, spread out enough so they could find some grass as they went. Pack them in too tight and the one's in front would trample everything down, let them spread too wide and you were running your horse's legs off trying to bring them back.

The first day, I wore out three horses. Mostly because I didn't know how to

do it right. Andy tried to help me out, but he had his own end of things to take care of. Old man Calhoun was riding back and forth along the side and he dropped back to help me out when he could. Somehow we got through the day, but by the time the herd was circled, I was worn completely to the nub.

Tired, I didn't pay much attention to supper and after quickly cleaning my tin plate, I rolled into my blankets and was asleep. It felt like only a few minutes later and someone was shaking me awake.

'Com' on boy, it's you turn to sing to the ladies,' the unseen rider growled.

Riding around the herd at a slow walk, humming a little and fighting to stay awake was the hardest part of my new job. By the time the sun started to lighten up the eastern sky, I was mad as hell at Andy. If he hadn't shot that dumb loud-mouthed kid, I'd still be working with Carl. I hadn't known how easy I had had it.

I missed working with the cook, but more, I missed his company. There was a lot of time we didn't talk much, but sitting a wagon bench all day was a lot better'n sitting a saddle. Freddy's saddle was pretty well worn out, but that didn't make it any better. Somewhat wider than the army saddle I'd got used to, it was heavier. Double cinched and with a saddle horn that was as big around as my upper arm, it was a lot more than any I'd ever sat in before. My leg seemed to fit the bigger saddle better and I was able to let the one stirrup leather out so my boot fit nicely. That helped me keep my balance when my horse would cut away unexpectedly to get alongside some idiot cow that wanted to drift.

Riding drag wasn't so bad. After the second or third day, it became easier. One of the reasons, I found out, was that all the horses knew what they was doing. All I had to do was squeeze with a knee and whatever horse I was on would turn sharply, heading at a quick

trot to the far side of any drifting cow. The horses were a lot smarter than the cattle.

The way things were broken up for riding guard, a rider only had to have a turn two out of three nights. After supper on the night I could sleep, I felt pretty good so I went to help Carl a little. He didn't say much, but when I chopped up a pile of fire wood and filled the water barrel, he did smile.

Flat Nose George had ridden in that day, bringing in two large deer carcasses, so supper had been fried venison steaks. George had nodded to me as he rode by and while I was helping Carl wash up the pots and pans, I said something about not having seen the Indian much lately.

Carl frowned and shook his head. 'George says there's too many people living around here. He has to go a lot further out to find any game. Probably a good thing we're getting close to Shreveport or we'd be cutting pieces of our saddles to fry up.'

'How far do you figure we are from that town?'

'Well, our faithful guide told Miz Mason that we're only three or four more days before making camp. I got enough coffee for that long, but I don't know about flour.'

I hadn't seen Capt. Holden since taking Freddy's place and that didn't bother me none. There was no reason for me to feel that way. Miz Mason had said once we were past Shreveport we were only another week or so from the ranch. The former army officer hadn't ever said two words to me, more'n likely hadn't even noticed me, so whatever the problem was, it had to be mine and not his. I figured I could put up with it for a couple more weeks.

Things went along like that for the next few days, eating dust all day while keeping the herd moving along and circle riding them at night to keep them calm and quiet.

The next thing that happened to break up the monotony took place one

night after supper. Carl had broiled the last of the venison and had made a pot of gravy to pour over his baking soda biscuits. Most of the hands were just sopping up the gravy and thinking about a cup of coffee when four riders came walking up out of the dark, rifles ready, warning everybody to sit still and not move.

At the time, I was just starting to wash up the pots and pans and had my arms elbow deep in the soapy water. The wash tub was on the wagon's tail gate so I was kinda out of sight of those fellas. From where I was, though, I could see that one of them was the guide, Capt. Sterling Holden. He was standing closest to me, with the others standing there pointing their rifles at the crew who was all just sitting there flabbergasted. From where I was, they were standing side to me so I couldn't make out the others.

'What's this all about, Captain?' Miz Mason asked.

'Well, missy, I'll tell you. There's a

cattle buyer waiting down at the loading pens just outside of Shreveport. He's there waiting to do a tally on your herd, so tomorrow we're gonna drive this herd down there and run them by him.'

'This herd's going to the ranch over in Texas. No reason for them to be tallied,' she said, shaking her head.

I had to agree, it didn't make no sense. Wiping the soap off my hands, I stood back there and listened. Every eyeball was on Holden and his three men and nobody was paying me any mind, probably didn't even know I was there.

Capt. Holden laughed, and pointed his rifle up toward the sky, placing the butt on his hip. With his feet spread out, he just laughed.

'Naw, missy. There's been a change in plans. You see, me'n the boys figure we can use the money for the sale of your cattle a lot better'n you.'

Calhoun, sitting on a piece of log that I had planned to chop up for firewood, put his supper plate on the ground next

to his feet. When he moved the two rifles swung over to point directly at him.

'Well, Captain,' he said. I'd never noticed before how slow and deliberate he talked, 'it's been taking half a dozen riders to keep that herd moving where we wanted it to go. How do you plan on getting it to those pens with only the four of you?'

'Now that's the beauty of my plan,' Holden said, still standing all relaxed. 'Miss Mason there will go for a ride with Howard,' he nodded to the man standing next to him, 'and he'll be keeping an eye on her. While she's off somewhere safe, you fellas will make the drive. Once the herd's all counted and we got the cash money in our hands, she'll be let go. Nobody does anything dumb and no one'll get hurt. Just keep in mind that the first person to be hurt will be the boss lady.'

That didn't set too well with anyone, but everyone could see they were helpless.

It was Andy that made the next move. He slowly finished sopping up the gravy and then, just as slow, while putting the piece of biscuit in his mouth, leaned over to put the plate on the ground. Sitting back up, he looked at the rifles pointing at him and shook his head.

Holden must not of thought he was a threat, since he went on talking. I wasn't paying any attention to what he was saying because I saw that Andy was staring at me. Watching him, I saw his hand slide a little toward his pistol and stop. Sitting there all relaxed, I didn't see how he could pull his gun and shoot all four of them. He'd be killed before he got the first shot off. But he must have had something in mind or he wouldn't have given me that look. I frowned.

Far as I could see, I was the only one the men wasn't pointing their guns at, but what could I do?

Now, my Pa had never said his only son was smart but then he never said I

was dumb either, but I coulda kicked myself for being so slow-witted that evening. Of course, my rifle was right there, under that pile of empty feed sacks. Thanks to Flat Nose George, it was loaded and ready to fire. Well.

Careful not to make any noise, I reached in and pulled the carbine clear. Standing as I was, I could see Andy was glancing my way so I nodded. He let a little smile cross his lips and nodded back.

All I had to do, I figured, was step out from the end of the wagon and shoot. That would give Andy time to get his pistol aworking. I'd shot men before, in the war, but I'd never shot anyone what wasn't expecting it. That's what I'd have to do now, step out and take my shot at men who was looking somewhere else. I didn't like that. Which one should I shoot?

Thinking about it a little, I decided I didn't like the idea of that Capt. Holden making off with Miz Mason and holding her hostage. No sir, I could

not let that happen. Glancing to see if Andy was ready, I saw he was. I nodded again, thumbed the safety off and stepped out and away from the wagon. Bringing the rifle to my shoulder, I didn't bother taking direct aim but lined up on Holden and fired. As quickly as I could, I levered another shell into the breech and taking better aim, fired again.

It is strange how everything seems to slow down in times like that. I suppose everything happened fast but I recall having time to see where my first bullet went, taking the former army officer in the chest, just below his right armpit. One of the other men was swinging around my way when my second shot hit him, knocking him back. There was a few other gunshots, from Andy I reckon, and it was over.

Holden and two of his men were down and the fourth was just standing there with his hands in the air, looking all pale and yelling about giving up. Andy shot him.

For a spell there was a lot of patting me'n Andy on the back. Carl made another pot of coffee and everybody sat around telling each other what had gone on. The things I remember most was when Miz Mason came over and put her hand on my arm and thanked me for what I'd done. That was the first time she'd looked at me, I guess. The other thing came to me after the coffee was gone and everyone had found their blankets and I was staring up at the stars and thinking about shooting that army captain. It dawned on me suddenly that nobody had finished washing the dishes.

14

Well, things settled down a little after that. From where I had stood and what I could see, maybe that last man standing was really just as dangerous as the others and maybe Andy was right in shooting him. Least ways nobody said anything about it. Except Carl, that is.

Holden and his partners had been buried in a single hole Carl and I dug off to one side of camp the next morning.

'I reckon that was one time,' he said when taking a breather and before we dropped the bodies into the dirt, 'when everybody was glad that you boys was with us. Andy worries me a mite, though, his willingness to shoot people more'n they really need. Don't know what we'd have done with that fella, though,' he said, using his shovel to point, 'probably a good thing he's

where he is, I reckon.'

That was pretty much all he said about it.

Riding drag didn't change much even though I was getting better at seeing when one or another ornery head was about to drift, often even before the dumb beast started to get out of line. Andy and me didn't have any time to talk about the shooting and I guess we really didn't have anything to say about it anyhow.

For the next few mornings, while eating dust and keeping the herd moving, I thought about the shooting a lot, finally deciding there wasn't much else any of us could have done.

Just as before, when we got near to Shreveport the herd was held some distance from town. It wasn't a real big town, at least the parts of it we saw. Carl turned down my offer to help him go in for supplies and when it came to going in for a drink I didn't go. Someone had to stay with the herd and I'd gone to town back in that little

farming town when others didn't. We'd made our halt at about noon and by nightfall most everyone was back in camp.

Listening to the talk around the campfire that night, nobody who'd spent the afternoon in town had much to say about it. Miz Mason said she thought we could probably take the herd the rest of the way to the Skillet without having someone point the way. She figured it was only another hundred miles or so.

Carl had said once that he figured the herd was moving about eight or ten miles a day, so that meant another week or two at the most. That gave me something else to think about while eating dust and pushing the herd. Andy had his family to go on looking for but I didn't. Wasn't no reason I could see to keep riding west with him. No reason not too, either, I guess. Except I was tired of worrying about him and the way he seemed to like shooting people.

I guess I wasn't the only one thinking

about what would happen when we got paid off. After helping Carl wash up after supper, I wandered off away from the campfire to sit and watch the stars, letting my supper settle, you know. I was laying flat on my back, sorta dozing, when Andy came over. He wanted to talk.

'Cletus, I been thinking about what the boss-lady said,' he sat down next to me. That was about the first time he'd sat so close to me in a long time. All I could do was wait to hear what he had on his mind.

'You know, I don't really have any good reason to go hunting up any of my kin folks. Remember that fella back at the home place saying he thought most everyone was going to Texas or maybe even up in the Indian Territory? Well, that covers a lot of country, I'd say. Not likely I'd find them, and even if I did, nothing would be different. I'd still have to start over, on my own. So I was thinking about staying on.'

I didn't say anything for a time, then

asked what he meant, staying on.

'Look at it, Cletus. I asked Homer about the Skillet ranch and he said that mostly there was only a few hands carried over the winter. Him and Slim, Calhoun and the Mexican kid and Carl was about all. They're all older, except for the Mexican and you can't count him. So I figure it'd be a good place for someone like me, young and a hard worker.'

Well, I couldn't argue with that. Far as I knew he was a hard worker and we being the same age, about, we was still young. At least younger than Carl and the others.

'Think on it, boy. That boss-lady is no beauty but she is for all that kinda fine looking. She's about the same age as me, I'd say. Now if I was to stay on at the ranch and play my cards right, well, who knows what might happen. The only young man around and she's getting to that age where women worry about becoming an old maid, I could end up marrying the boss's daughter.'

He lay back with his arms folded behind his head, just like I was, and stared up at the stars, both thinking about what he had said.

He was probably right. It was a chance for him to make something of himself. Of course, neither of us knew much about it; just maybe she already had a beau back there. I didn't say anything, not wanting to cause him any trouble, but I thought it was quite likely she was or had been courted, probably by someone from that town near the ranch.

After a while I got up and said something about getting a cup of coffee before turning in.

The herd was swum across the river that bordered Shreveport. Carl explained to me that it was the Red River. Swimming a couple of hundred head across that river, even when it was down, was a chore, let me tell you. Cattle just don't take to water naturally. Even the horses didn't like it much. I could understand that, seeing as how I didn't like it either.

I didn't have a compass or any feeling about direction, but even I could see by where the sun come up in the morning that we were heading a little more north. Since joining the herd, I saw we'd been going toward the west, riding into the sunset. Now the sun was setting off my horse's left shoulder. I hoped someone knew where we were going.

For the next few days things went along the same way, riding drag all day and circling the herd at night. Always getting closer to the end of the trail.

The next time something happened was a night I didn't have any night riding to do. That night, after turning the horse I'd been riding over to the Mexican, I went down to the little creek Carl had camped by to wash some of the dust off. Early night out there on the prairie was a special time. After spending all the day in the saddle, watching the rear ends of a bunch of cattle, my ears full of dust and their bawling, the quiet of the night was

more noticeable. I'd used my kerchief to wash the dust off my neck and I was just standing there, looking up at the sky full of stars and listening to the quiet, when Miz Mason walked up.

'It's a beauty, isn't it?' she asked, standing right next to me. 'I do love being out here, away from the herd, where it's all quiet and still.'

I couldn't think of anything to say. There hadn't been too many girls back home. Oh, of course there was those sisters of Andy's, but they was little kids. At school the only girls I could remember was the Pike girls. Just like their brother, Piggy Pike, they was butt-ugly, what with their noses broad and smashed back and all. No, this was the closest I'd been to a girl as I could remember. And this wasn't just a girl, she was a woman and the boss at that.

'Uh huh,' was all I could think to say.

'Cletus, I followed you out here because I wanted to talk a little with you. You don't mind, do you?'

'Huh, no, ma'am, I was just washing

up a little. Trying to get some of that dust off.' I thought I was stammering so stopped talking.

'The thing is, I figure we're about five or six days out from the ranch. You and your friend, Andy, and most of the others will be paid off once the herd's on Skillet grass. Father doesn't keep many hands through the winter, so there'll only be Homer, Slim and Carl staying on. I wondered what your plans are?'

'Well, Miz Mason, to tell the truth, I don't know. It's something I've been giving some thought to, but don't have an answer right now.'

'Now, I don't want to cause any trouble between you and your partner but I'd like you to think about staying on,' she said and then quickly held up a hand before I could say anything. The stars gave off some light, but the moon hadn't come up yet so most of what I could see when I looked at her was just white dim shapes. I was able to see her hand, though, stopping me from talking. 'You understand that it would be

Father who would be the one to offer you the job. I can't do that, but I can suggest it to him and he usually trusts my judgement.'

'Why, Miz Mason,' I said after a long minute of silence, 'I don't know what to say. Shoot, I don't know anything about cattle or horses, for that matter. Pa and me, well, before he died, we had us a farm. I can plow a straight furrow and plant a crop of corn, but everything I know about livestock is what I've learnt here, and that's just how to keep the herd moving.'

'Cletus, none of us knew anything about raising cattle until we had to learn. Look at Carl, there. He was a good rider until a horse fell on him. He had to learn how to cook, didn't he?'

All I could do is shake my head. 'How come you was to pick me? Andy there, he's probably a lot smarter than me. Did you ask him, too?'

In the weak starlight I could see her head drop as she looked down. 'No,' she said softly. Then looking up, she

went on, 'I don't want to make trouble for you, but, well, I just don't trust his judgement. No, I haven't asked him and I'd appreciate it if you didn't mention that I've talked to you, either.'

I wondered what she meant, not trusting his judgement and guessed it had to do with the shooting of that third man. Thinking about what she said, I guessed I wouldn't say anything about what Andy had been talking about.

'The only person I've talked to about asking you,' she continued, 'is Carl. He agreed with me that of anyone in the crew, you were most likely the best to hire if I could.'

'Shoot, Miz Mason, even Juan knows more about horses and cattle than I do. How come you don't keep him on?'

'Oh, he's staying. Juan and his family have been at the ranch since we first started. His mother takes care of the house and his father is the yard man, keeping the barn and house in order. And Flat Nose George is there most of

the time, too. He hunts some and goes off to his people at times, but he always comes back.'

I did some quick counting. 'That leaves only me'n Andy out, and you say you're not asking him.'

Slowly, with her head once more down, she shook her head. 'That's right. I just don't think Andy would work out, that's all.'

'I don't know what to say, Miz Mason. Guess I'll have to think on it.'

'Do that. We have about a week until we're on the ranch property. But please, don't say anything to Andy about it, alright? I don't want to hurt him and make your life miserable in case you decide to keep riding.'

I could see that was the best thing to do, so I nodded. 'All right, but I do thank you for thinking of me.'

'It was the way you handled that Captain Holden that set me thinking. When I talked to Carl about it, he told me how you help him out even when you don't have to. I think you'd make a

good job of it, working at the ranch.'

'Well, we'll see.'

'Yes. Now, I'd better get back before someone notices how long I've been gone.'

In the dark I wasn't sure, but it looked like she gave me a smile before hurrying off. Now that was something to think about.

15

I still don't know exactly what made Carl know when the herd was on Skillet range. Just as Miz Mason said, about a week after she'd talked with me, we were there.

The first I knew about it was when Homer came riding back to wave Andy and me aside.

'You can stop pushing them, now,' he said, a big smile on his face. Homer was someone who'd lived most of his life outdoors. The skin on his face was sun and wind burned, all coffee colored and looking like leather. You could tell he was old, though. Some of the wrinkles that lined his face were so deep your finger would sink to the first knuckle if you was to poke at them. But for all of that, when he smiled, his teeth flashed white and almost pearly.

'Come on,' he waved us on, 'Carl

already has the wagon up at the main house.'

Me and Andy just sat there a minute, looking at each other and then kicked our horses into a gallop, following behind Homer. Riding up a slight rise, he kept going but when we got there, we reined back and stopped. There below was the ranch, a white painted house running longways with a red barn to one side and a series of corrals behind that. On the other side, boxing in the front yard of the main house, was a string of smaller houses; I counted five of them and one long narrow house, all painted white. A creek ran from somewhere up behind all these buildings, curving back behind the white houses. The chuck wagon was sitting in front of the main house.

Looking back over my shoulder, I could see that the herd we'd been shoving all those days were spreading out, chomping at the clumps of grass, not paying any attention to anything. They'd likely already forgotten about

being driven from way back there to here. I didn't think I'd ever forget it.

As you might recall, there was a celebration that night. All I expected was to be paid off but that wasn't what happened. First everyone stood around, shaking hands with the boss, not Miz Mason but her pa, Alexander Mason. Then, I don't know who started it, probably Homer, but we were all herded toward the long bunkhouse.

Out back of the bunkhouse, that long narrow building I'd seen from the ridge, was a long horse trough-looking tub. Just like a bunch of boys playing in the swimming hole, the crew used that tub to take a real bath. Real because there was a couple bars of some kind of sweet-smelling soap to wash with. That wasn't the first tub bath I'd ever had, but the best one.

After we put on our cleanest shirts and went on back out to the front yard. While we was getting clean a couple of long tables had been placed in front of the main house. Chairs and dishes and

such were all laid out. Later I was told that Juan's mother, Graciela, had been cooking and baking for two days, getting ready for this welcoming home meal.

Me and Andy were really the only newcomers. I wasn't sure how to do things so I just watched how the others did it and followed along. The beef had been cooked over a big pit full of hot coals and was sliced nice and thin. There was corn on the cob, roasted potatoes and lots of fresh-baked biscuits. The gravy that I poured over nearly everything was the best I'd ever tasted.

Everybody laughed when someone commented on how much better this supper was compared to what we'd been eating and maybe, before ever making such a trip again, Carl should ought to take some cooking lessons. I don't think Carl took it seriously, because he laughed too.

There was a few bottles of wine on the table, but after tasting it I decided

I'd stick with water. Andy liked the red liquor, though, and drank the rest of my glass of the stuff. After supper, everyone sat around on the veranda and talked, telling stories of what the drive had been like. It wasn't as if we hadn't all been there, but it was still fun to hear. Nothing much was said about the shooting, neither when Freddy was killed or when that Capt. Holden tried to take the herd. Mostly it was just good story telling.

We all bedded down in the bunk-house that night. There was a pot-bellied stove in the middle with bunks lining both walls. A lot more beds than there were men, so there was enough for Andy and me.

After breakfast the next morning, we were mostly all standing around one of the corrals looking over the horses that was milling around in there, when Carl was called over to the big house. He came back a bit later.

'Well, boys, here it is. Mister Mason is going to take us all into town for a

drink,' he stopped and looked around at all the faces, 'and while we're enjoying ourselves, he'll go see about getting the money from the bank to pay us. Boys, it's payday.'

Well, that made everybody happy. Of course, it also made me think about what me'n Andy was going to do. All during the ride in to town, that's all I could think about.

16

Riding behind a herd of cattle all day makes it hard to find time to look up and see how blue the sky is. Listening to the bawling of those animals as they shuffle along makes the sound of a bird call sound strange. Hell's bells, even the quiet talk among the men me and Andy was following into town was out of the ordinary, at least to me. I'd gotten so used to riding drag that this ride seemed like a holiday.

It was a nice day, the weather was good with a soft cool breeze blowing under a cloudless sky. Hearing a bird's song, unseen in a stand of stunted pines off to one side of the wagon road, made my head snap around. It'd been a time since I heard something like that. That only brought it home, how quiet it was. Now, don't get the idea all of the boys were just riding along, hands in their

pockets, so to speak. No sir, there was a lot of foolishness going on. No, it was because there wasn't any long string of cattle ahead of us and because there wasn't much talk between me and Andy. Neither of us had much to say, I guess. I know that thinking about the offer of a job that Miz Mason had talked to me about made saying anything to my partner difficult.

Nobody had said anything more to me about that job, though. It was likely that the offer wouldn't be mentioned again. If it was, well, I didn't know what I'd do.

I needn't have worried. As it turned out, Andy was offered a job in town even before we got paid.

The boss and Homer had dropped off at the bank, inside there at the general store, and the rest of us rode on down the street a ways. The saloon didn't really have a name. Or at least there wasn't any sign outside pointing to where the business was. Carl and the others, they knew where they was going, though.

Inside the place made me think of that last saloon me'n Andy had been in, back there where Andy had shot Freddy. Guess you see one saloon, you've seen them all. Fact is, those barrels holding up the planks that was the bar could have been the very same ones there in that little farming town's drinking establishment. Even the bartender looked the same, short and bald, holding a dingy bar rag in one hand, watching as the Skillet crew came trooping in.

'Well, look who's here,' the barkeep howled even though there wasn't but a couple other fellas in the room. 'Carl, you've been gone a bit and I gotta tell you, it's been right quiet around here without you.'

That got a laugh from nearly everyone. I guess the joke was that Carl wasn't the kind of man who'd make a lot of talk. A quiet sort of fella, you know. The same could be said for Slim and the others, too. Of course, what did I know? I'd only see them out there on

the trail, not inside and liquored up. They all could be different then.

'Where you boys been?' the bartender asked as he set out a stubby little whiskey glass in front of every one of us. Without asking what we'd have, he just poured a brownish liquid from a bottle into each glass. The bottle didn't have any label as far as I could see.

'Ah, hell, Sammy, you know where we been,' Carl said, picking up the glass and holding it up to the light.

'Yeah, I guess,' Sammy nodded, still holding the bottle, waiting for everyone to drink down their drink. 'I'd heard you and the boys went on over toward Mississippi, bringing back a good-sized herd. Now what's old Mason got in mind, anyhow? There's a whole passel of unbranded stock roaming around out there on the flats. Haven't been anyone in these parts to burn a brand on them, not since the war.'

'Come on,' someone called from the other end of the bar. Slim, I think it was. 'Stop your standing around and

pour some more of that homemade bug juice.'

'Now, don't go talking down this fine liquor,' Sammy said, moving quickly down to top up the small glass. 'You gotta admit, it's sure a lot better'n not having any at all.' That got a groan from most of the crew lining the planks.

'Well, I guess old man Mason knows what he's doing, but I certainly don't.'

'Sammy, that's why he's out there making money on that piece of ground and you're in here pouring rot-gut whiskey. The critters that're out there running around wild aren't much for butchering. They're mostly all just skin and bones and appetite. Those animals we went over across the big river to get are a different breed from the longhorns. Mr Mason plans on improving what herd he's been keeping back so he can sell to those northern meat packing plants.'

'What? He's going to send cattle to the Yankees what just not too long ago whupped the Confederacy?

'Hey, Sammy, ain't you heard?' someone else piped up, 'Us southerner's lost that war. Now we're all going to get along with each other.'

'And let's not be refighting that war, either,' a loud, hard sounding voice cut in. I had been leaning back against the planks, but when I heard the newcomer, I just naturally whipped around to see who'd come in.

The man standing just inside the doorway was a big man, standing a good foot taller than my five and a half feet. His voice may have sounded mean and angry, but the smile on his face made a liar out of it. Tall he was but it sure didn't look like he'd missed any meals lately. I'll wager he weighed in at pretty near 250 pounds. A shiny silver star hung from the pocket. I glanced at Andy to see if he noticed.

'Hey, Sheriff,' said Carl, standing down on the other side of where Andy was standing, 'we know all about the war. We got us two real live Confederacy soldiers here.' Putting a hand on

Andy's shoulder, he smiled at the big lawman.

'And let me tell you, it was a good thing, back there on the trail, that they had joined up with us, too. Four gents thought they were about to take our herd from us. Thanks to Andy here, and his partner Cletus, that didn't happen. Boys, this here is Sheriff Caulfield, Toledo's big upholder of the law.'

'Well, you're not the first of the southern soldiers to be coming into town, but you didn't miss it by much. Boys, welcome to Toledo,' the sheriff said, a smile a yard wide curving his lips. He shook hands first with Andy and when he took my hand I thought I'd never held such a huge bunch of fingers. 'Carl, what's this about someone taking your herd?'

'Come on over here and get comfortable around this table, Sheriff, and I'll tell you all about it,' Carl waved the lawman away from the bar.

'What do you think, Cletus,' Andy asked, putting his head close to mine.

'Are we far enough away from that little bit of trouble that was following us back there in Vicksburg?'

'I reckon,' I said, watching Carl and the big man settle into chairs at a table over against a wall. It wasn't likely the law here in Texas would find out about something that happened back there, I decided, and turned back to my whiskey.

I didn't like the taste of it much and when the bartender came my way again I asked if he had beer.

'Sure do. Make it myself and it's about the best you'll find in this part of the state,' the short man laughed.

'That's only because it's the only beer brewed in this part of the state,' Slim joined in the laughter, 'Sammy, don't lie to these boys.'

The beer was pretty good, not cold of course, and kinda yeasty, but drinkable. I wiped the foam from my lip and glanced over to where Carl was sitting. The two men had their heads close together.

The talk along the bar settled into quiet conversation as we waited for the boss to bring our pay. Andy was sipping his second or maybe third whiskey when Carl called out for him.

'Hey, Andy, come on over here. I might have a deal for you.'

Andy quickly looked at me and then squaring his shoulders a bit, picked up his glass and sauntered over to the table. I thought it was probably the whiskey working that caused him to put a little swagger into his walk. I was still on my first glass of beer, making it last, and all I could do was watch as Andy pulled a chair and sat down.

About that time, Homer came in, holding up a sack and yelling, 'Here it is, boys, payday for the best bunch of drovers this side of . . . well, this side of the river. The old man's gone on to fill out the list that Miz Mason gave him, so I'm the paymaster today,' he said to groans from the bar.

Setting down at a table, he started counting out stacks of gold coins.

Taking a tally book from his shirt pocket, he called for the men one name at a time. I stood, nursing my beer, waiting for my name to be called. It was the next to the last one.

'Cletus, I was told to add this bonus to the pay you and your partner earned,' he said, handing me a nice little pile of the beauties. 'Now look here, the boss is over at the store, like I said. How about you walk on over there and have a word with him.'

He wanted to talk to me away from Andy, that was what it was about, I told myself. I still didn't know whether that's what I wanted to do, though. Nodding to Homer, I went back to put my empty beer glass on the bar when Andy called to me.

'Hey, Cletus, guess what?' he asked, a big smile on his face. It wasn't, I saw, the cold hard smile I'd seen too much of, though. 'Sheriff Caulfield here has offered me the deputy sheriff's job. Says with all these out-of-luck soldiers coming through town he needs some

help. Can you see that, me toting a badge?'

I could see it pleased him no end. Glancing over at Carl, I saw how he'd worked it. Now I could see no problem with going to work out on the Mason ranch.

* * *

Well, I reckon that takes us up to about where we are now. You know the rest of my story. It's no big secret what happened next. At least everybody thinks they know what happened next, but I can tell you, they don't know the half of it. And if anyone should be told the whole story, I suppose it's you. So here goes.

That herd of cattle we'd brought in hadn't even been road branded. Of course being a farmer I didn't know anything about road branding a herd when moving it across a lot of country. All those critters still carried the brand of the previous owner. Carl said Homer

208

had decided it wasn't worth it, to take the time to mark that brand out and put on the Skillet brand. So that was the first job we was given.

The branding took us most of that week and Homer figured we'd be done with it with a couple more days. We didn't work on Sunday. After sitting around the bunkhouse, resting up and washing our clothes and such that day, we was back at it on the first of the next week. The men who'd come out from town just kept riding when we came in late on Saturday. They were going to spend their day off at home, I reckon. Anyway, it was one of them, a man called Gus Moon, who told us when he came riding back just about daylight on Monday all about how Sheriff Caulfield had been fired.

Seems a bunch of Union soldiers had come riding into town and just took over. Moon said they even kicked the mayor out of his office over at the courthouse. That caused a lot of talk among the rest of the crew. It made me

think of what had happened back at Choctaw when that Union government man, Bullock, had taken over. Thinking about that made me a little uneasy about Andy and his new job of deputy sheriff.

I didn't have a chance to ask Moon about Andy until later in the day. He said he hadn't heard anything about any deputy sheriff. Since leaving him in town, I hadn't thought much about Andy but now I was back to worrying about him. It still scared me to think that what the war had done to him, making him so quick to shoot people, might have been done to me too.

17

Tell you the truth, I couldn't hardly believe it when I found out what had happened. We'd finished up with the branding and Homer and me took off and spent the next three days riding the range. He wanted me to see where the ranch boundaries were and at the same time check out the four line shacks that were used in winter.

The ranch wasn't fenced and when the winter storms hit there wasn't any way to keep the cattle from drifting. Sure and they were all branded big as day, the outline of the Skillet burned into the left flank of every head, but that didn't mean much to some people, Homer said. That's mostly what the hands would be doing over the coming winter months, staying in the far-flung cabins and riding out from there to push back any critters that had taken to roam.

There was a growing market for beef back east, he explained as we rode out one morning in the middle of the week.

'Right now the price of prime beef is pretty good back east,' Homer went on talking, poking a heel in the side of his horse to continue on with our ride, 'all those folks hungry after living it thin during the war. It helps having some kind of cousin or something up there owning the meat packing plant. Mr Mason's got one and so he's got one of the contracts to supply the beef.'

Riding along at a fast walk with Homer telling me about where things were, like a pond over near the bluff or the creek that'd been dammed up, making a water hole that was good all summer long no matter how hot it got. But I don't guess I got to tell you about that.

Anyway, he was saying that was what the drive had been for, new breed to build up the ranch herd for sale to the eastern market. He said there was already a contract with some big

packing plant up in Kansas for next spring's herd. We'd pulled up to the top of a rolling hill and sat taking in the wide, mostly flat land below us. But I wasn't thinking too much about the country or even about the future of the cattle we saw here and there during our ride. For the most part I was worried about what trouble Andy was in lately.

On one hand, I knew it didn't have anything to do with me any more, no matter what it was. But then he had been my partner and about the only person I knew from home.

After a while, when I didn't ask any questions or say anything, he stopped talking. Except when pointing out something he thought I should know about.

'Look over there,' he said once, pointing toward what I thought was probably west. 'See that little black dot moving there?'

Well, I even stood in the stirrup and held up a hand to shade my eyes, but all I could see was a few head of beef and a

whole lot of brush. No moving dot of any color anywhere. Far off, the purple-blue of a mountain range reached up into the lighter blue of the sky.

'I would think that's probably Flat Nose George coming back to the ranch. His people have their summer lodges up in those mountains back there.'

George had left the ranch soon as we came in with the herd and hadn't been back since. Someone said that's what he did, ride out to be with his family for a while and then come back when it got too much for him.

'He'll likely be meeting up with us at the Soda Springs line shack,' Homer said, gigging his horse again. He said we'd spend that night at the Soda Springs cabin, the Big Flats cabin the next and back at the ranch late the next day.

Homer was right. George was at the shack when we rode in that evening. He stood in the open doorway, nodding when we pulled into the yard, then without saying anything, turned back

into the black of the room. We pulled the leather from our horses and turned them out into the corral where they got to rolling in the dirt, cleaning off the day's sweat, I figured.

Both the line shacks I'd seen were the same, a lot like the house me'n Pa had had. Three walls built tight up against the dirt hillside, the fourth wall having been dug into the hill. Bunks built along two walls, enough to sleep four people, a rough plank table and four or five low-backed chairs and a flat-topped cast-iron wood stove against the back wall was all the furniture. George had a fire going and the coffee pot on when we came in.

'Well, George,' Homer said, tossing his bedroll onto one of the bunks, 'had enough of the mountains?'

'Enough, yeah,' was all the Indian said.

I laid out my blankets and went back out to the bucket of water on a bench next to the open door. Splashing water over my face and hands, I was using a

dingy thin towel to dry off when I heard George say something about Andy.

'What's that?' I hurried back into the cabin. 'You talking about Andy?'

From all the times I had seen George, I could never recall him smiling or changing the still expression on his face. This time was no different. He just looked at me a long minute and then nodded.

'I was in town and hear he now works for the new boss.'

Homer stopped and looked up as he poured three cups of coffee. 'What'd they do, hire another sheriff? I never did figure why old Sheriff Caulfield was fired.'

'Yeah,' George went on, still looking right at me. 'New marshal is from government. New mayor, too. Your friend Andy rides with the marshal.'

That sounded to me a lot like it was in Choctaw and LeFleur's Bluff, the Union government bringing in their own law.

'You sure?' I asked. It would be hard

216

to believe Andy would ride with that kind of deal after what had happened with his family.

'Yeah. Everybody angry at the marshal. Running people from their ranches. Stores in town closed, too.'

Homer frowned. 'What do you mean, running people off their places. Why would anyone do that?'

George didn't answer, just shook his head.

'Taxes,' I explained. 'The Union government is making people pay extra taxes and if they don't, their farms and businesses are auctioned off. Andy's pa's place went like that. George, you're sure he's helping them?'

George's expression didn't change and his black eyes continued to stare into mine.

'Yeah. People saying the marshal went to get taxes from Spencer family and the Spencer boy got mad and got his rifle.' He stopped talking.

'Hey, I know the Spencer's,' Homer said. 'They got a little horse breeding

217

place down south of Toledo a piece. A good family, three boys as I recall. It must be the oldest one what you say got his rifle. He always was a hot-headed boy.'

George didn't say anything, and his eyes didn't waver. Finally I had to ask. I didn't want to, but I had to know I was wrong.

'What happened when he got his rifle?'

I wasn't wrong. George shook his head slowly.

'Friend Andy shot him,' he said then turned away to pick up his coffee cup.

18

Nothing much else was said about it. George rode on the next morning. I don't know where he was going and he didn't say. Me'n Homer rode on, with him pointing out landmarks and places the cattle liked to go. Most of those places were down in coulees and narrow ravines.

We spent the next night at the line shack on the far side of what Homer called the Big Flats. Getting back to the ranch, we settled in to what I learned was the normal work, fixing what fences had been put up, cleaning out the water holes and such. Anyway, there were a lot of little jobs that kept us busy for the next couple weeks so it was close to a month and a half before we had a chance to go to town. I had been looking forward to that, hoping to have a talk with Andy.

Even in the saloon, the bartender wasn't happy like he'd been that time before. Wasn't nobody I could see doing a lot of smiling. But I did get to meet up with Andy. He was looking good.

'Seems like you made out all right,' I said looking him over. We'd taken a couple chairs on the wide porch in front of the hotel and he was leaning back on two chair legs with his boots up on the railing. The boots, I saw, was new riding boots with the high heels that I'd noticed most cowboys wore.

'Well, Cletus, you got it right. When they fired old Caulfield I figured I was gone but no, the new marshal asked me to stay on. They're paying me more than Caulfield did, too. Naturally I spent some on new pants and such. Got to look prosperous to be prosperous, I'd say.'

I waited but he didn't say anything else about his job so I had to ask.

'Andy, what exactly is it you're doing for this marshal? We've been hearing that the Union man is collecting taxes,

just like what was done back there in Choctaw.'

He smiled and nodded. 'Yeah, it's a lot the same, I reckon. Look, Cletus, it's the way things are. The south lost the war, and that's all there is to it. Ranchers'n farmers and such have to pay the taxes and that's our job, the marshal and me. Seeing that everyone pays up what they have to.'

'Seems hard. And it doesn't sound like something you'd be interested in helping them do. I mean, that's what happened to your family place, wasn't it? The Union man chasing your pa off his land and then ending up owning it? Doesn't seem like it's fair.'

'No, boy, but that's the way of it. There was winners and losers in that war, and we lost. Now I could just keep travelling but sooner or later there'd be a government agent coming wherever I was, just like here. All right, if that's the way of it, and I'm offered good money to help out the winners, then I'll take the money.'

'But what about that shooting over at the Spencer's farm. Did you have to kill that boy?'

'You weren't there, were you,' Andy was instantly angry like I'd never seen him before. 'No, so you don't know, but that boy was just as dangerous with his rifle as if he'd been a full-grown man. I reckon I did what I had to do. That's what I'm paid to do, help the marshal do his job.'

For a spell we just sat and watched people as they went about their business. After a while, smiling once again, he glanced in my direction.

'Anyway, you don't have to worry any about it. The Mason ranch is not on the list for the extra war taxes.'

I didn't understand that. 'What do you mean? Why is the ranch left off any list?'

'Well, it seems that Mason is contracting to supply the north with beef. He's got the backing of someone pretty important up there who's got him excused. So we both are places that

won't be hurt by the Union government. All we got to do is our job and we'll both be wearing new boots.'

I'd already thought about making some purchases while I was in town, but now I wasn't so sure. Somehow it didn't seem right for us to be going along so happy while others was losing their homes and farms. It didn't bother Andy to be part of the Union tax collecting and I wasn't sure how much it bothered me to be working for a ranch that somehow had a free pass to the taxes everyone else had to pay.

That was about all we had time to talk. Andy was due to ride out with the marshal and had to be saddling up the horses. We didn't even have time to get a drink together, but I guess that was all right, too.

Sitting there that afternoon, thinking about Andy and the Union taxes and things, I finally decided he was probably right. Whether I wore new pants and boots and went on working for a ranch that didn't have to pay the

taxes didn't really matter. It didn't change anything. What Andy was doing was different, though. But that was something he'd have to work out for himself. Once again I had to tell myself I wasn't his partner any more and wasn't his keeper. Hell's fire, I never had been.

I went on over to the general store and bought a pair of riding boots.

* * *

For the next few weeks there wasn't much news coming from town. Work at the ranch took on an everyday sameness. Most nights, being tired, I'd simply drop into my bunk after supper. One evening, not being so tired, after bathing in the water trough out back of the bunkhouse and taking a round of joshing from the rest of the hands at supper, I wandered out to look at the stars. What I was doing was getting away from more teasing, but it was good out there on the ridge above the

ranch buildings, sitting under the night sky. It reminded me of when we was driving the herd and watching the stars when riding night guard. And then I remembered the night Miz Mason came out and talked to me about maybe staying on the ranch.

I hadn't seen much of her since hiring on. Once in a while she'd come down to the corral when we was working the horses, and there'd been a time when she asked me if I'd saddle a pinto pony she liked. But that was about all.

It was while I was sitting up on that little rise, watching the full moon coming up over the far dark mountains that I remembered that night she came out of camp to talk to me. Smiling a bit, it seemed part of my thoughts to hear someone coming through the tall grass. Glancing back down toward the lighted windows of the buildings, I saw her coming up to where I was.

'Hey there, Cletus,' her voice was just as soft and calm as I recalled it had been.

'Ma'am,' was about all I could think of saying.

'Now, let's get past that right off. My name is Sally, not ma'am or Miz Mason. Sally.'

The moon had that big fullness that it seems to get when seen out on the open grasslands. Her face in the moonlight was almost like when seen during the day, only softer somehow. I remembered what Andy had said that time, how she wasn't all that beautiful but was not a mud fence, either. In the moonlight I thought she looked pretty good.

'All right then, Sally,' I finally agreed, even if it didn't sound right coming from me.

'I was watching you working on that sorrel this afternoon. Remember when we talked about you maybe staying on after the cattle drive? You said all you knew was farming. Well, it looks like you're starting to learn a bit more about cattle and horses.'

It was a good thing, even with all that

moonlight, that she couldn't see me clearly 'cause I was all hot faced and blushing. All I could do was nod, something else she probably couldn't see.

That was about all I recall of that night. We sat and talked, with her doing most of the talking, for I don't know how long. Nobody said anything to me when I came into the bunkhouse and crawled into my blankets. Maybe they was all asleep and didn't notice.

The work went on and neither Miz Mason, uh, Sally, or I went for any more night walks. At least I didn't. Then one day a couple riders came out from town, checking to see if there was any work to be had. Slim and I were helping Juan's pa shoe up a bunch of horses when they came riding in.

Antonio, Juan's pa, was working the forge that was in a lean-to built onto one side of the barn. Slim and me would bring a horse in and he and Juan would work at replacing the shoes if it was needed. Not all did, but when all

four had to be changed then we just sat on the top corral bar and watched. Antonio was good at what he was doing, using a heavy hammer to shape the red-hot horseshoe to fit each horse.

That's where we were sitting when the men from town came over. For a time they just stood there, leaning on the corral rail, watching Antonio work.

'Say,' one of them said, looking up at me, 'you're the fella what rode in with that deputy marshal, ain't you?'

'You mean Andy? Yeah,' I nodded, not taking my eyes off the shoeing that was going on. I didn't want to talk about my old partner and certainly didn't want to hear anything new about him. That wasn't to be.

'Well, I don't want to ruffle your feathers none, but it wasn't a good day when he arrived. You folks out here been hearing what's going on around the country?'

I decided not to answer. I didn't want to know. Slim did, though, and answered. I wouldn't even look around.

One of the strangers cussed and the other went on to tell us the latest news.

'He's shot three or four more men, from what we've heard. Hey, Slim, you remember that wheat farmer out east, the place along Dead Man Creek? Name of Collen, a tall, skinny man living by hisself. Well from what we heard, he told the marshal he wasn't about to pay any Union taxes. That Yankee lawman claims Collen pulled a pistol and his deputy had to shoot him. There've been other cases like that, too.'

'Yeah, folks are complaining,' the other man added, 'saying that deputy is too quick with his revolver. That damn Yankee what calls himself the mayor says he's the district judge and he'll be the one to say when the marshal or his deputy is not doing his job. I don't know what's going to happen, but there's been some talk.' He didn't say anything more for a minute and I glanced over at him. Both were looking right at me.

'I'd say,' the one man said after a bit,

'it wouldn't surprise me if someone was to get mad enough about all that shooting to do some themselves.' I didn't move or say anything. He quickly went on, 'I don't know about any of that, but there's talk, that's all I'll say.'

All I could do is look away. I wasn't my partner's keeper and never had been.

The two riders didn't come to work then, but was told to come around in a couple weeks when we'd start moving the cattle off the flats and pushing them toward the protection of the foothills.

There was always enough work around a ranch, I learned. All the hands would be out right after breakfast, usually just as the sun was coming over the horizon, and few would be back unsaddling before the sun was near to setting. A week or so after taking my walk up to the ridge to watch the moon come up, I decided after supper one night to walk up that way again. I hadn't been paying any attention and didn't see her until I got to about that

same place. Miz Mason was there, sitting with her knees drawn up, sorta hugging them close.

We sat there and talked some more. It was a moonless night, that time, and it seemed to be extra quiet, maybe because of that. Whatever the reason, our words were kept low, almost as if we didn't want to disturb anything. What we talked about I couldn't tell you, we just talked as two people will.

I remembered at one point, I guess it was when we was walking back down toward the house, what Andy had said back on the drive. When he was thinking about maybe asking for a job at the Skillet, saying how the owner's daughter was young and all the hands was old and maybe she was lonely. That thought came up but I pushed it away quick as I could and tried to never think about it again.

After that time, it happened again a few nights later, the two of us getting together up there to talk. It got so I was looking forward to those little meetings.

I found myself telling her things about me that I hadn't ever told anyone before, not even Andy. More, I have to admit now, that I've added to this story, too.

I liked working at the ranch. The work was hard but it felt good, too. Homer, Slim and everyone treated me good, just like I was one of them. Even Flat Nose George stopped simply staring at me and once in a while, whenever he was there, would speak to me. Juan and his pa and their family were friendly and I was learning more and more of that Mexican talk. Sunday's were always good days, most times there'd be a barbeque with Juan's ma and pa cooking up something good. Those last days of summer were some of the best I could remember.

It all ended when Andy came riding into the yard one evening, his horse hard ridden and all lathered with thick foamy sweat.

19

'We got trouble, Cletus,' he yammered as he swung down out of the saddle. The horse, a black with three white stockings, stood where it stopped, head hanging and breathing in big gulps.

'Andy, you like to kill that horse, riding it that way. What's so important that you'd treat an animal like that?' I'd never seen him so, all sweaty himself, just standing there with the reins held loosely in one hand.

'Come on, you can tell me what's bothering you while we walk the horse. You don't cool him down he'll never be any good for anything any more.'

I might not have known much about cattle, or horses for that matter, but after learning from Pa how to take care of his mules I knew you couldn't just let the overworked beast stand there. Anyway, walking let us get a way from

any of the other hands that might have wandered by.

It was easy to see that he was troubled even though I couldn't recall ever seeing him like that. Hell's fire, this was the first time he didn't look like he knew what he was doing.

'All right,' I said when we got a ways off from anyone, 'what's happened that you came clear out here to the ranch?'

'Here,' he said, stopping and taking a folded up piece of paper from his hip pocket. 'It came in with a stack of them this morning.'

I took the paper and noticed it was showing some signs of wet along one side, probably from sweat leaking through Andy's pants, so I slowly and carefully opened it up so as not to tear it. I saw it was a Wanted poster.

That stopped me in my tracks.

'What're we gonna do, Cletus?' I'd never heard Andy ask that kind of question before. I held it up at arm's length, I read the big black type across the top of the page. Wanted, it said. The

line under that simply said, The Wilson Brothers. That didn't make any sense to me, I looked over at Andy, frowning.

'Read it. It's certain they're talking about us. See, here,' he pointed about halfway down. There wasn't a picture like there sometimes was on wanted posters but someone had sketched in two men's heads, one was a fella who had a really high forehead, no hair growing until you reached the top of his head. I started reading what it said below that.

'These two men are wanted by the Union Governor of Jackson, Louisiana. Thought to be brothers, the two are wanted for the dishonorable shooting of Governor Obadiah Bullock, appointed official for the community of Choctaw, and Clarence Pike, the legally elected Sheriff of that same community in May of this year. One of the killers has a healed bullet wound above his forehead and the other killer's right leg is unbending at the knee. These two men were last seen in the town of Vicksburg

soon after the dastardly killing of the two officials. A reward of $500 in gold is being offered for their capture.'

At the very bottom of the poster in the same big black words as above were the words, 'Dead or Alive'. Reading that made me feel all clammy and sweaty.

I read the writing on the poster twice more and then started walking the horse again. I didn't say anything for a while, trying to figure out how that Vicksburg marshal had come to think different of us. I guess it didn't really matter. More importantly, they was still looking for the Wilson's, not anyone named Wilkins. Slowly folding the poster back up, I handed it back to Andy.

'Where'd this come from, Andy?'

'It came in this morning's mail. There was a whole stack of them Wanted posters. The marshal told me to look through them so I'd maybe recognize if any of those wanted men was to come into Toledo. I was supposed to tack them up on the wall

outside the office door. When I saw that one and read it, I quickly folded it up and got my horse.' He was walking along, his head hanging down, chin almost on his chest, just like the horse.

'Well, it's clear that Vicksburg marshal had time to think about it some. Wonder why he didn't mention that the two he thought was the Wilson's was heading toward Texas. He was right quick to point us outa town, remember?'

'Yeah. I dunno why. Cletus, do you think anybody seeing that poster will recognize us as being them? I mean it's damn hard to hide that stiff leg of yours. I can keep my hat on so my head's covered. Don't often take it off anyways.'

I shook my head but didn't say anything. Here he was, asking me what to do. That showed how scared he really was.

'No,' I answered after a while, 'I'd say it was unlikely anyone would, even with my leg sticking out. Most anyone who's seen me don't notice that stiff leg after

a while, I don't think.'

We walked a little more, not talking. Without meaning to, we'd been walking a big circle and was coming back near the corral where Slim and Juan and the others was working those horses into shape. I angled away and led Andy's horse to the small corral where I'd been working.

'Was they any more of these posters with the Wilson's name on them?'

'No, there was only one of each. That's all there ever is. We get a stack of them every couple weeks. That Union marshal says the government is putting up a lot of money for rewards to keep people from shooting the officials that're sent out to collect taxes.'

'Well, then if you destroy that poster, then nobody'd see it will they. And if you keep a watch out for any others that come along, then we're home safe, I'd say.'

Andy didn't say anything for a long moment. 'You know, that drawing don't look nothing like us, Cletus. I reckon

you're right; ain't nobody gonna take another look at us if they don't see the poster. Here,' he handed it back to me, 'you burn it or tear it up or something.'

I could drop it in the stove in the bunkhouse and nobody'd notice.

Andy was a lot more relaxed now, enough that he even chuckled. 'Hey, think on it, Cletus, we're pretty bad outlaws. It's not everybody that's got such a big reward being offered for them. In good Yankee gold, too.' He sounded almost proud of it.

'Well, you better forget all about that. Now, this horse isn't going to take you all the way back to town. Let's go see if we can get a Skillet horse for you. Someone'll bring this one of yours in the next time they come in.'

I asked Juan and he found one of the ranch horses that wasn't going to be used in the coming roundup. Helping Andy strip the saddle from the black, I thought it was probably a good time to ask him about the stories I'd heard.

'Hey, Andy. There's talk that you've

shot a few people when they couldn't pay up the Union's taxes. Any truth to that?'

'Well, yeah. I've had to put down a few folks, mostly them what didn't see what was right there before their eyes. Some people just don't realize that when the South lost the war, that gives leave for the Union government to take some kind of control. Anyway, if I didn't do it, the Union marshal would just find someone else to do his dirty work and I'd be out of a job.' Swinging up into the saddle he looked down at me and smiled that familiar smile, the one that didn't ever reach his eyes. 'You got it good out here, Cletus. Hell, you know I don't know anything about ranching. I couldn't get a job like you got. Working for the government's officials is all I can do.'

I dropped my hand and stepped back a bit. 'I seem to recall a fella that chased us off your family farm saying about the same thing.'

Andy chuckled, 'Yeah, and look what

it got him. No, this is different. Now, you get rid of that poster and we'll forget all about it, all right?'

Now that the threat seemed over, he was back in charge of things. I was damn glad to have a place like the Skillet. Shoveling horse manure wasn't all that bad.

20

Pushing the herd out of the flat land and getting them going toward the thin, forested foothills was easy work. Long hours in the saddle, but mostly it was just chasing them up outa the little grassy places they'd been used to. Once they got to moving, the dumb animals would likely keep going, pulling a mouthful of grass to munch as they ambled along.

Then the next morning, the same thing, getting them started. Riding back and forth, making as clean a sweep as you could.

Most of the nights I was by myself in one of the line shacks but it wasn't long before I figured I was close enough to ride in to the ranch. A few times I was so late getting in, Carl had to reheat whatever it was he'd fixed the other hands for supper.

Thinking back, those were the best nights of that season. Getting in and turning my horse string over to Juan or his little brother, then having supper. After the first night, when I was too tired to do more'n just fall into my bunk, I took to taking a little walk up on the ridge top to look at the stars. Sally often came out for a walk, too.

She hadn't been putting her hair in a tight bun like she'd done when on the drive. Since that ended, she'd let her hair hang down as it normally would. I thought it looked good, hanging down and floating around her head. It made her face look a lot softer and somehow friendlier. Nicer, I guess.

I'd gotten past calling her Miz Mason. We was getting to be good friends. No, we were getting to be real good friends. That was something else, she was real nice about telling me how to use words better. One night she asked me if I could read and when I said yes, she offered to let me borrow a couple of her books. She said if I read

them it wouldn't be long before I started talking and using words the way they was, uh, were supposed to be used.

Well, I always thought as long as someone, anyone, I was talking too understood what I was saying then I was talking all right. She said there were right ways of doing things, and wrong ways. There were a lot of things like that I didn't know and things she taught me.

As I said, those were real pleasant nights. The days were long and I'm not exactly sure we got all the cattle from the flats up into the low hills where they'd be more protected but Homer said he thought we got the most of them. Come the spring, he said, we'd be surprised how many head we had to ship up to the packing plant.

The first frost of the season came on and I was in town buying some winter clothes the next time I got to talk with Andy. There hadn't been any more stories about him shooting people, least ways any that I heard. When I saw him, though, he wasn't like he usually was,

all happy and friendly. He was a lot like when he found that Wanted poster, all white faced and sort of skitterish, if you know what I mean.

That's what I asked him, 'Andy, did another of those posters show up?'

'Huh? Oh, no. No I've been very careful to be the first one in the office whenever it's time for another batch of them to be coming in. They send them from someplace up north just about every three weeks. No, it ain't that.'

'Well, then, what's bothering you? When you left the ranch you was, uh, were feeling pretty good. Telling jokes, even. I didn't think joking about having a big reward hanging around our necks was something to joke about, but you were.'

'No, Cletus, that isn't it. This is something else. I was sent with a buggy over to Texarkana to the railhead there to pick up a Mister Thomas. He's some big shot what's the boss of all the Union officials in this part of the country. Can't ride no horse, so I had

to go over to bring him back. He'd ridden the train down from Little Rock, the marshal said.'

'So, what'd this big government man do that was so bad?'

'Nothing. It wasn't him that's causing me some worry. It's a fella I think I saw over there in Texarkana. Someone I think I recognize. I ain't sure and it's been bothering me something fierce.'

'Who would that be, Andy. Someone from the army? We ain't, uh, haven't anyone chasing us from the army, have we?' The way I used 'ain't' was another of those words that Sally was against. Now that is one I certainly don't understand why she could not be in favour of. But she is and it seems like she's more against it than nearly any other. Maybe this is all part of her being female, I don't know.

'No. Cletus, you remember that Pike family. Clarence Pike what we called Piggy Pike? You recall if he had any younger brothers?'

Now that caused me to frown, trying

to remember back to those days. There'd been a lot of water under the bridge since then.

'Let's see, there was Clarence, who was about our age, and you were the one who first called him Piggy if I remember right. I seem to recall a couple younger sisters he had. They were true Pike's, their noses all pushed back. I can't be sure about any brothers, though. Certainly could have been, I suppose. Hell's fire, I don't even remember any of your kin and I was over visiting more than I'd ever would of gone down to the Pike's place. Their place was clear down to the other side of Choctaw, wasn't it?'

'Yeah.'

'So, is that who you think you saw, a Pike?'

'Uh huh. That's who it looked like, the nose was like that, wide and sorta turned up so the nostrils are looking at you. He didn't see me and I didn't get a real close look at him. I was pretty busy getting that government man settled in

the buggy. He's a real dude, I tell you. 'Are we likely to see any Indians?' he wanted to know. 'Is that the only weapon we've got, that pistol? What happens if there are road agents?' Gawd, he never relaxed that entire trip back here. I'm hoping the marshal will take him back to catch his train. That man's afraid of his own shadow, I swear.'

All I could do was shake my head. 'I doubt whether it was a Pike you saw. Anyway, what difference would it make? You certainly don't get to Texarkana all that often. I think that's where we're going to be driving a small herd next spring, to the railhead there for shipment north to the packing plant.'

'Yeah, that's what the marshal said. He wanted to go out to the Skillet to collect taxes but that man, Mister Thomas, he was very clear when he said there'd be no causing the Mason's any trouble. The cattle he's going to ship north is too important. Mason's not the only one, either. There's a few other

cattlemen whose names are on a list that we're supposed to stay away from. That's all right by me. I certainly don't want to cause you any trouble.'

'Doesn't seem right, but I guess that's the way of it. What're you going to do about it if that was a Pike back up there in Texarkana?'

'Nothing, I guess. Probably like you said, has nothing to do with Pike or me at all.'

Well, that was the end of our talk. I bought a couple of pairs of pants, the heavy canvas kind, and a long wooly coat. I also spent twenty dollars on a new Stetson. Boy, that was something. I'll have to work on the wide brim to get it to curl the right way.

Riding back to the ranch gave me a lot of time to think about what Andy had said. It seemed like he was getting boogered easier all the time. I don't think when I left him he felt much better about the fella over in Texarkana that might have been a Pike. First it was that Wanted poster and now a Pike.

Maybe his conscience was starting to get to him. I mean, I had shot that guide, Capt. Holden, and a few others, mostly during the war, and I didn't stay awake at night thinking about them. But he'd killed a lot of others that maybe didn't need killing. And that could be, like that preacher me'n Pa had gone to hear said, weighing on his soul.

What with the poster, and now maybe a Pike coming to bother Andy, even having Andy as he was, a shooter for the Union marshal, perhaps it was time to make some decisions.

Until recently I hadn't thought too much about what I was going to do. I was pretty happy just letting things take care of themselves. They always had, even after Pa died. But things were different now. Riding along, I made up my mind. It was time to be thinking about getting married.

21

I didn't ride out with the rest of the crew the next day. Instead I waited until they had all gone to wherever Homer had them working. Right after breakfast I told the foreman that I wanted to talk with the boss. Homer had just nodded and went on giving everybody their marching orders. After the hands had all gone their way, I slicked back my hair, squared my shoulders and went up to the main house to do as I said, to talk with the boss, Alexander Mason.

* * *

It was Antonio's wife, Graciela, who answered when Cletus had knocked on the front door that morning. The mother of Juan and his brother, Antonito, Graciela often worked as the housekeeper in the main house.

251

'*Sí*, Señor Cletus,' the tiny brown-skinned woman said, her teeth flashing white in her smile. A small woman standing at least a foot shorter than the young cowboy, he found himself looking down at the top of her head.

'Uh, yeah. Good morning.' Cletus had been learning a lot of the Mexican talk from working around this woman's husband, Antonio, and from her son, Juan. Coming face to face with her so unexpectedly though, he wasn't able to remember one of the words he'd learned. 'Uh, I'd like to talk with the boss, Mr Mason,' he said, hoping he wasn't stammering.

When he had decided to front the head man that morning, he hadn't given any thought to who would be likely to open the door. Now, thinking about it, he was glad it hadn't been Sally.

'*Sí*, señor. Would you be so kind as to wait here in the front room and I will see if Señor Mason is finished with his breakfast.' Throwing up another smile

at the young man, she disappeared through a beaded curtain that covered a doorway in the far wall.

Cletus, standing hat in hand, found himself in the front room of the big house. It wasn't the first time he'd ever been in that room; the first time had been right after taking on the job. Mason had invited him to come up to the main house, said he wanted to meet the new hand in person. That one time wasn't enough to make the young man feel at ease, though. He had been so nervous that he hadn't noticed anything.

The house seemed to him to be empty, it was so quiet. When Graciela came through the beaded curtain, it was the first sound he'd heard since he'd come in.

'Señor Mason will be here in a moment, Señor. He asked if you would make yourself comfortable,' she waved a hand toward one of the dark wood chairs. Cletus nodded and, still holding his hat, now in both hands, gingerly sat

down on the cushioned seat.

Leaning back, he felt himself relax a little. It was somehow restful, he thought, a lot like sitting on a feather mattress, one with a back to lean against.

The housekeeper had turned back toward the beaded curtain but stopped when Mason came through. Mostly, during the time he'd been working on the ranch, Cletus hadn't seen too much of the boss. Standing next to the chair he'd been sitting in, he now had a chance to study the rancher a little.

Mason wasn't a young man, but he hadn't been out in the sun and wind all day, every day, like Homer or Carl or Slim. His face was brown, of course; you couldn't live long in this country without being in the sun somewhat. Even Cletus had noticed that his skin was browning just like everyone's, except where his hat and clothes covered him up.

He wasn't so young but he wasn't so old either. To look at him, Cletus

thought he was a lot younger than his Pa had been. But then his Pa had had a tough life and the worry he'd had to carry had probably aged him some. Anyway, Alexander Mason stood square-shouldered and he stood tall. It was clear, the young cowboy thought, he was the boss of his own house, a successful man and probably a contented man.

Finished with whatever he wanted to tell Graciela, he smiled down at her and then, as she left the room, came over to Cletus, putting his hand out.

That bewildered the young man; it wasn't likely the ranch owner would greet a hired hand like that.

'Good morning, Cletus. Graciela tells me you asked to talk with me. Please,' waving a hand toward the cushioned chair he went on, 'make yourself comfortable,' he said before taking the chair across from his visitor.

Cletus, still trying to get over his nervousness at being greeted almost like a guest, sat back down. For a bit

both men simply looked at each other, not saying anything. Mason was still smiling a little, Cletus saw. It wasn't much of a smile, the young man noted, but it was there. Just awaiting to find out what this was all about, Cletus guessed, not so willing now to begin. Hell's fire, he thought, he didn't even know where to begin, but it had to be done.

'Well, sir, I guess the thing for me to do is just start in. I do thank you for taking the time for me this morning, but I've got a long story to tell you.' And that started it, the flow of words that seemed to take forever to get through.

* * *

Finished, Cletus stopped and waited, hoping, like he said, that the older man would see how it was important and that he understood. Again, like before Cletus started to tell his story, the two just sat and looked at each other for a long minute.

'Well, there you have it, Mr Mason, that's the story. I guess, like I said way back at the beginning, if ever anyone should hear all about me, it's you. When I started I didn't think it'd take this long, and for that I'm plumb sorry. But I still think it's only fair.'

Mason didn't say anything for a long minute, just sat there looking at the young man.

'Now yes, I'd agree, that was quite a speech,' Mason said after a bit. 'Even though it's still early in the day, I think we both could use a small drink. Your throat must be dry.'

Not giving Cletus a chance to turn it down, Mason went to the table and poured a little whiskey into two glasses. Coming back and handing one to the younger man, he sat back down and nodded.

'Now, tell me what this is all about.'

Cletus took a tiny sip and carefully placed the glass on the low table.

'Well, sir, it's like this. I come from a family that most of us didn't even know

257

our own last name. We didn't have much and after Ma died we seemed to have even less. What we did have a lot of was hard work. So that's about what I have to offer, hard work. Now, this is a new country, I've heard Carl tell me that more times than I can count. He says Texas is going to grow, now that the war's over. And it's going to need young, hard-working men. So that's me again. I know that isn't much, but I have grown to feel strongly about your daughter, Sally, and I think she feels the same about me. Sir, I'm asking your permission to ask her to marry me.'

There, he thought, feeling almost relieved, it was said. Picking up the glass, he tossed back whiskey. He hadn't wanted anything to blur his thinking that morning and was glad the rancher hadn't offered him a drink earlier. Now though, it was all over. Now all he could do is wait.

Sitting there, after he'd put the empty glass back onto the table, the thought crossed his mind that he hadn't

seen or heard anything of Sally. He wasn't even sure she was in the house. The frown that thought brought to his thinking hadn't even really started when he heard a horse come galloping into the ranch yard.

'What the — ?' Mason said, getting up and going to the window.

'It isn't one of the men,' he said after pushing aside one of the lace-edged curtains. 'That's one of the horses from O'Keefe's livery. I recognize it 'cause we sold it to him a year or so back.'

'Hey, anyone here?' the rider called out, not getting out of the saddle.

Mason pulled open the front door and stepped out onto the veranda with Cletus right behind him.

'Hey, Cletus, your friend's been shot.'

'What friend,' Cletus answered and even before the rider said anything, he knew.

'That deputy that's been working for the Yankees, Andy Wilkins. I reckon someone finally had enough of that

highbinder's ways. Anyhow, I came out to tell you 'cause you'n him seem to be so friendly.' Cletus thought the rider was getting too much fun out of telling him the news.

'Is he dead?'

'Yep, sure is.'

'Who shot him?'

'Dunno, some stranger. Ugly looking fella, too. Looks like someone mashed his nose back again his face and it didn't pop back out when it healed. Now look, I did what I was asked to do, come out and tell you. Now I'm going on up toward Scully's place. He's putting me on to take some kinks outa a string he's going to winter over. Wrong time of year for it, I say. Better to let them stay rough until spring and then get 'em used to the saddle again, but if he wants to pay me, I'll do it.' Waving his hat, the rider reined around and rode on out of the yard.

For a minute Cletus just stood there thinking, then, not taking the time to even glance at Mason, he ran for the

corral. Pulling a rope from a saddle that'd been left hanging over the top rail, he quickly dropped a noose out and just like he'd learned how, flipped it over the head of the nearest horse. Cinching up the saddle, he swung aboard and was out of the yard, not looking back so he didn't see that Sally had joined her father on the veranda steps.

'What's that all about, father? Where's Cletus off to in such a rush?'

'Seems that partner of his, Andy, has been shot and killed. From what he told me this morning, I can't for the life of me see why he's so quick to go riding out, though.'

Sally watched as the young rider made the corner down by the creek and went out of sight. 'Father, whatever the reason, it must be important to him. I'm going into town.'

Alexander Mason stood there a bit, thinking, before nodding. 'Let me hitch up the buggy. It'll take a little longer but not much. There isn't any great rush anyway, far as I can see.'

* * *

Cletus had to fight back the urge to kick his horse into a run. It wouldn't do any good, he knew, to flounder the animal. Keeping to a steady trot, he had time to think things out. If it was who he thought it was, and going by that rider's description it had to be a Pike, it had to be the one Andy thought he'd seen over in Texarkana. The only reason he'd be after Andy would be because of Andy having killed his brother, Clarence. That meant, according to the Wanted poster, that Andy's stiff-legged partner would also be on the Pike list of revenge. That didn't leave Cletus many choices. Thinking about it there on the steps, he could only see two. He could head out and hope to stay ahead of him or he could go face him now. The chances of Pike being satisfied with shooting down Andy and letting Cletus go were bound to be damn slim. Either choice, he knew, meant his plans for the future were any longer possible. He

couldn't ask Sally to run with him and he certainly couldn't just sit around and wait for Pike to come looking for him. No, better to go in and face it now.

At least, he told himself, this all came to a head before he and the girl was married. That is, if they was, uh, were, ever going to get married. Alexander Mason hadn't said whether he approved or not. Now it wouldn't matter much.

22

It was coming on noon when Cletus rode into town, so the first place he went to look for Pike was the Mexican's. There weren't many places a man could go get a bite to eat in Toledo and the Mexican's was one of the more popular. That was mostly because it was cheap, not that the food was that good.

There were those who wouldn't eat at the Mexican's, believing the lack of stray dogs or cats in town could be attributed to him. Cletus didn't think any of the Pike clan would worry about something like that. But there was no Pike or anyone who looked like a Pike there. That left only one place for someone who'd just killed a lawman and wasn't in jail to go, unless he had already left town: the Lone Star Saloon. Cletus didn't think Pike figured he was finished in this part of Texas.

The Lone Star Saloon was where the Skillet crew had celebrated the end of the cattle drive and where Andy had been talked into taking the deputy's job. Back then, the place didn't have a name but now there was a newly painted sign hanging over the front. Painted in big letters, it let everyone know, this was The Lone Star Saloon.

Anyone spending any time in the middle of the day, and was holding up his own as far as drinking was concerned, for a nickel would be allowed to dig into the big plate of sliced ham, cheese, hard-boiled eggs and pickles that was put out at the end of the bar. Even on the hottest summer day, one of those when there was no breeze and the sun beat out of a pale blue sky hot enough to bake the ground brick hot, inside the Lone Star was always cool.

Cletus hadn't thought of himself as being an honest-to-goodness cowboy yet. After all he'd only been on the Skillet a few months, but, just as any

cowboy would, he came out of the Mexican's and got back in the saddle to ride the half block down to the Lone Star.

Pulling up to the hitch rack in front of the saloon he sat for a minute thinking. Horses were tied to both the two hitch rails out front leaving no room for another. A half dozen or so more were tied to the porch railing. For some reason this was a busy day for the drinking establishment and the only reason Cletus could think of for that was the killing of the deputy marshal. Andy, he knew, hadn't been highly thought of anywhere in the area.

Now it takes a good man to know his limitations and then, in a time of stress, to act on them. There were some men in his position who would have barreled right in, six-gun blazing. If he was smart, he'd get two six-guns. But as certain as a bear makes piles of yesterday's meal in the woods, that man would soon be very dead. Cletus knew his limitations. He was no hand with a

rope or a six-shooter.

Busting in the swinging doors wasn't very smart either. He'd be coming in from the sun-bright street into the dark cavern of the saloon. It was that fact that made it so special during the heat of day, little sunlight ever got through the windows that had been painted over, and so very little heat from that sun made it either. Anyway, there wasn't anyplace to tie up his horse.

Lifting the reins, Cletus gigged his horse down the narrow alley between the building that housed the saloon and the single-storey shack next door. Blue Tooth Alice had a room in that shack as did Lota Bright Wing, who was the offspring of a Cree Indian warrior and the wife of a white missionary, or so she said. Neither of those two ladies paid any attention to Cletus riding slowly down the alley. The two men being entertained by the two ladies had other things on their minds.

At the rear of the saloon Cletus tied the reins to a stunted tree that grew

right next to the shaded wall, close by the back door. Climbing down, he pulled the rifle from the saddle scabbard and quickly checked to make sure it was loaded. That rifle was the same Sharps carbine that Andy had given him way back there in Choctaw. It was a good weapon and short, only a little longer than a man's arm, and shot a robust .54-calibre bullet. Pulling back the big mule-ear hammer, he let the rifle hang, his right finger on the trigger and reached for the door knob, then stopped.

Standing there along side his horse he shook his head. What was he doing? He asked himself silently. Wasn't this just like something Andy would do, going in to shoot someone? Was he just like Andy after all?

For a minute he thought about getting back in the saddle and riding away. Everything he wanted was here; Sally, honest work among good people, and maybe someday his own family. And he was throwing it all away to

avenge his partner, a man who most certainly was going to be shot down sooner or later anyway. Maybe he was a lot like Andy had been.

He didn't like it, but it had to be done.

Not giving himself time to change his mind, he slowly pulled the door open and stepped into the gloom of a back room. Before closing the door behind him and blocking out the sunlight, Cletus saw piles of wood boxes that were filled with brown bottles. A large wooden vat sat on low sawhorses and whatever was fermenting inside was bubbling.

For a moment, while he let his eyes adjust, that was the only sound. Then, in a burst of laugher, sounds from the saloon itself took over.

Easing open the inner door a thin crack he looked out into the main room. Without opening it any more, he had a clear view down the bar, the portly bartender on one side and a bunch of men on the other. Cletus

thought long and hard but couldn't recall the barkeepers name.

The men standing with their backs to him lined the bar, all looking farther down. From the noise of the talk, it seemed they were listening to a loud voice giving a speech or maybe, he thought, preaching a sermon. Looking out, he waited, trying to catch the words.

'Well, that's the way of it, boys,' the preacher said. Cletus thought from the sound of it the man was happy with himself. 'That Andy Wilkins and my brother were enemies from the first day they met.'

It was a Pike that was talking. Standing there bragging to a bunch of dumb townies about the man he'd killed. 'You know how it goes. For some reason, none that anyone can explain, two people will just take a dislike to each other. They were young'uns, I don't recall how old. Hell's bells, I was only a tadpole myself. But they fought there at that school every time they saw

one another. Clarence, my brother, was a good student, Ma said. I don't remember much about that. By the time I was old enough that I could keep in mind things like that, the school had already closed down. Couldn't find a teacher, as I recall. Anyway, that Andy Wilkins was a bad 'un, always picking on the girls and then calling people names.'

Cletus frowned at what he was hearing and almost stepped out to make a few corrections, but then decided to wait a little. No reason, he thought, to rush into things.

'Now,' Pike went on, 'you all know that saying, sticks and stones can break bones, but words can never harm you? Well, we all know that ain't exactly true. Call someone a dirty, nasty name and pretty soon, why it just does something to him. That's what happened to Clarence, I reckon. He'd fight with Andy and I'm certain he'd flatten him too, make him eat those bad names he was using, but for the fact that Andy

had a friend. Yes sir, hard to believe anyone'd stand up for a scoundrel like that, but one fella did. My brother told me. It was Little Cletus Cooper. His pa had a farm up the creek a piece, just beyond the Wilkins's place.'

That did it. That was enough. No longer listening, and still holding the carbine down along his pants leg, Cletus pulled open the door until he was standing square in the doorway. From where he stood he couldn't see anything but the backs of those listening to Pike's rantings, at least the ones on this side.

Taking a deep breath, Cletus called out, cutting Pike's words in mid sentence.

'Hey, Piggy Pike.'

The silence that fell in the room was deep as a still mountain pool. Then someone looking over his shoulder to see who was making all the noise saw Cletus standing there and quickly jumped aside. In the time it took to let out a deep breath, everyone had moved,

leaving a big, stout-looking man standing alone at the bar, one hand raised as if he was about to start another argument.

'Piggy Pike, that's what Andy and all the kids at school called that ugly son of a brother of your'n,' Cletus said, letting his voice drop. 'It's clear, just looking at you, anyone can see where the name come from.'

This Pike was a lot like the one Andy had shot in Bullock's office so long ago. A big man, but round shoulders and tubby looking. The fingers on the end of that arm still pointing to the ceiling were short, stubby sausages. Cletus could clearly see his beady little eyes, a lot like when Ma was making cookies and poking raisins into the dough before putting them in the oven to bake.

'What — ' Pike quickly looked to see where every one had gone. Then seeing the man in the doorway, he appeared to realize the danger he was in. Slowly letting down his arm, he hooked a

thumb over his belt inches away from the butt of a holstered pistol. Most of the belt was buried by his stomach which hung down over the buckle. Cletus wondered if there was a buckle under it all.

'What the hell you talking about? Who the hell are you?'

'Don't you recognize me, Pike? I certainly knew right off you were a Pike. You got that same piggy snout for a nose that all Pike's have. Piggy Pike, that's what Andy called your brother back there in school. You don't know me? Why, from all the brag I been hearing you make, I thought it would be a cinch you'd know me. I'm Cletus, Piggy Pike, Little Cletus, to hear you tell it. I can't figure out where that came from, but you're right. It was one of the last things your fat, ugly brother said before Andy shot him.'

The silence in the room was complete, not even the sound of heavy breathing broke the stillness.

'Well, Piggy,' Cletus was feeling

pretty good. Now he knew he was doing this for himself, not to avenge anyone, and he felt good about it. 'Old Andy upset a lot of people around here and I can understand that. But for you to shoot him, well, you must have come up behind him or something.'

'No,' Pike's voice was loud, almost yelling his denial. 'He was there when I saw him, I called his name and he turned, pulling at his handgun but I was ready. He killed my brother.'

Pike's hand slipped toward his gun butt as he talked. Cletus didn't say anything, just lifted the barrel of his carbine and touched the trigger. The big rifle slug took the chubby man square, flinging him backward.

23

Cletus, the rifle pointing at the floor once again, stood with his shoulders sagging, looking at the man lying on the saloon floor. Somehow, the body that had been round and flabby had kind of flattened out and now looked all empty. Cletus didn't feel as good about things as he had a minute or two before.

'Now, dammit, it was a fair shooting,' he heard someone yell and realized there was an argument going on with the bar crowd.

'Don't matter,' another disagreed almost as loudly, 'this Pike fella did us a good turn, getting rid of that Yankee murdering cuss. I say this shooting wasn't right. That man there's a killer and oughta be hung.'

'We can't hang anyone,' a third angry voice cut in. 'Maybe that Wilkins was a killer and maybe he died as he should,

according to what the Good Book has to say about it anyway, but that don't mean we can just up and hang a man what had shot another fair and square. That'd make us killers our ownselves.'

Cletus didn't really care. He'd stepped over to the very end of the dark wood bar and was standing by himself, almost ignored by the argumentative crowd, none of which was within ten feet of him, almost as if he were a leper and they were afraid of catching something.

'Here comes that Yankee marshal,' Cletus heard someone warn. 'Let's see what he has to say.'

'Yeah, after all, it was his man that this fella on the floor shot in the first place. You know what,' the speaker paused a bit, 'this dead man's nose does look somewhat like that big old hog of yours, Clements.' A few of the men at the bar laughed at that, but only a few.

Cletus laid the rifle on the top of the bar and was thinking about ordering a glass of beer when he saw the crowd

open up to let the marshal get close to Pike's body. Standing directly behind the lawman were Alexander Mason and Sally.

'Well,' the Yankee marshal said, his northern accent sounding hard and curt, 'he's dead, no doubt about it. Now, then, who's willing to tell me what this shooting is all about?'

At once a dozen or so men started talking. Cletus, still undecided whether he really cared, turned to lean against the bar, looking empty-eyed at the shelves of bottles that lined the wall.

'Now wait a minute,' the lawman's voice rose up, bringing silence back to the crowd. 'Will only one of you do the telling? All I'm interested in at this point is whether this shooting is something to take before the judge. Now, who is it going to be?'

'Uh, Marshall,' Cletus heard Alexander Mason speak out, his voice sounding softer coming as it did right after the marshal. 'We heard enough when we came in to know this was a

clear case of self-defense.' Instantly, a few of the closer witnesses wanted to disagree.

'No, hear me out,' Mason's voice rose above the spectators. 'You all heard it. This gunfight started a long time ago. It was almost, you might say, the end of a feud, a personal battle that started even before the war and a long way from Texas.'

Again, a number of lookers-on wanted to differ with him.

'Wait a minute, boys,' Mason wasn't giving up. 'Think about what you all heard here today and what happened yesterday. Yes, there's no question that that former member of the Confederate Army might have deserved to be hanged after doing the dirty work of this Yankee marshal.' Cletus didn't look, but he figured those words wouldn't earn him any pats on the back from the northern lawman. 'That is as it may be, gentlemen. But times have changed. Right now the Union government is running things, but that won't last

forever. We're all Texicans and no Texican will put up with that kind of behavior long.'

These words brought a cheer from the crowd. Maybe Alexander Mason was giving warning to the marshal, Cletus didn't know. Mason wasn't through, though.

'This stranger lying here on the saloon floor didn't shoot Andy just because Andy needed killing. No sir, we heard it from his own mouth. He was called out because he'd killed this man's brother a ways back over there somewhere in Louisiana. So what happens? He stands here telling you all lies, accusing that fine young man down there at the end of the bar, himself a hero of the Battle of Spanish Fort. What could Cletus do? What would any Texican do? Yes, he's new to the country, but he is the kind of man this new country will need.'

Cletus wanted to smile and was about to look around to see how all this was going down when someone touched

his arm. Glancing down, he found Sally looking up at him. She had let her hair down and it swirled around her head, gently touching the smooth skin of her neck, a few curls brushing her tiny ears. A soft smile played with her lips.

'Come on, Cletus,' she said looking directly into his eyes, 'let's go home.'

Which is what they did.

THE END

GONE TO TEXAS

Andy and Cletus, wounded late in the Civil War, flee the battlefield and head for home ... but Yankee carpetbaggers have taken over. Andy's family has been evicted from their ranch, so he turns to what he learned in the war: how to kill. The enemies now are Yankee politicians who came south to loot and plunder. When 'Wanted' posters circulate, however, the two friends join a cattle drive going to Texas, but the brutal past finally catches up with them.